THE R
SCH

CW00326290

Student Textbook

Effective Soul-Winning and Evangelism

Effective Soul-Winning and Evangelism
Student Textbook

Reinhard Bonnke
with Dr. Mark Rutland and Dr. Gordon Miller

English USA

Copyright © E-R Productions LLC 2008
ISBN 978-1-933106-68-7

Edition 1, Printing 1
10,000 copies

All Scripture quotations are taken from the King James Version of the Bible

Editor: Teresa Düppmann

Literary Production: Reinhard Bonnke
Compilation: Dr. Mark Rutland, Dr. Gordon Miller
Cover Design: Isabelle Brasche
Typeset: Roland Senkel
Photographs: Rob Birkbeck

Published by:

E-R Productions LLC
P.O. Box 593647
Orlando, Florida 32859
U.S.A.

www.e-r-productions.com

For further information on the world-wide ministry of
Christ for all Nations, on E-R Productions LLC,
or for details of other publications,
please contact the address above.

Printed in China

Brief Contents

Overview of Topics

Module I

Module I

Module II

Module III

Module IV

Module IV

Foreword

Since the start of the new millennium, through a host of major events in Africa and other parts of the world and with a goal of seeing **100 million souls record a decision for Jesus Christ** in this decade, more than **44 million people have already responded to the Gospel** call during the *Christ for all Nations* Gospel Campaigns. In addition, **1.3 million pastors, missionaries, and church workers have attended the *CfaN* Fire Conferences worldwide.**

These conferences have stirred a strong passion for saving souls in hundreds of thousands of Christians, resulting in an amazing impact on whole countries and nations. **Millions have been set ablaze for God.** Multiplied thousands have been inspired to greater dimensions of evangelism and ministry. Motivation and mobilization for soul-winning – this is the purpose of the CfaN Fire Conferences and the Reinhard Bonnke **School of Fire.**

The Reinhard Bonnke School of Fire

The inspiration which created such zeal for soul-winning is now captured for Christian's everywhere in **the Reinhard Bonnke School of Fire** studies. The *School of Fire* is global instruction for unity of action in the Great Commission of Jesus Christ. It serves to teach personal evangelism and corporate evangelistic outreaches.

It is our goal to undergird the burning desire to win souls for Jesus Christ by profound theological teaching. Through our courses and studies on effective soul-winning, we equip students with Biblical knowledge and principles of evangelism that will turn the call, the desire and the anointing to evangelize into effective action. It is our mission to train evangelists who step out and go into the world burning with a passion for the lost and applying what they have learned, thus winning precious souls for Jesus Christ.

Through the **School of Fire** we are able to pass on what the Lord has entrusted to me in decades of evangelistic experience. This is an exciting and wonderful opportunity to extend the Kingdom of God. **We have to relearn how to reach the lost, so that Jesus can save them!**

Evangelist Reinhard Bonnke, Founder

Introduction

Welcome to this *Reinhard Bonnke School of Fire* study on effective soul-winning and evangelism! Thank you for partnering with us in reaching the lost with the Word and compassion of Jesus Christ.

You are about to engage in an exciting and challenging study that will inspire and refresh your faith. It will provide you with practical and encouraging teaching, and it will inflame you with a passion for soul-winning. Make this study a priority in your life and join passionate soul-winners and evangelists all over the world who have become effective "fishers of men". Soul-winning is the noblest task of the Church of Jesus Christ until he returns and YOU can have a significant part in it!

Authors

The teachings and reading material provided for you in this study are based on the expertise and the knowledge that the Lord has entrusted to Evangelist Reinhard Bonnke over decades of effective evangelism and which Reinhard Bonnke has put into writing in 4 books.

Using other unpublished texts and material by Reinhard Bonnke in addition, the reading material has been created in cooperation with Dr. Mark Rutland and Dr. Gordon Miller from Southeastern University in Lakeland, Florida.

We would like to thank Dr. Mark Rutland and Dr. Gordon Miller for their cooperation and excellent work in putting this study together.

Study Material

The reading material for this School of Fire study consists of

* this Student Textbook
* corresponding passages from 4 books
  by Evangelist Reinhard Bonnke
* texts from the Bible

Each of the 20 lessons in this Student Textbook consists of reading material that is based on texts by Evangelist Reinhard Bonnke. Whereas lessons 1 and 2, which serve as an introduction to the subsequent lessons, have been written by Evangelist Reinhard Bonnke, lessons 3 through 20 have been compiled in cooperation with *Southeastern University.*

In addition to the reading material in this Student Textbook, passages from the following 4 books by Evangelist Reinhard Bonnke need to be read for lessons 3 through 20.

Reinhard Bonnke: *Evangelism By Fire*
                      Full Flame GmbH ©2002, Edition 8
                      Frankfurt, Germany

Reinhard Bonnke: *Mighty Manifestations*
                      Full Flame GmbH ©2002, Edition 2
                      Frankfurt, Germany

Reinhard Bonnke: *Faith - The Link With God's Power*
                      Full Flame GmbH ©2003, Edition 7
                      Frankfurt, Germany

Reinhard Bonnke: *Time Is Running Out*
                      Full Flame GmbH ©2003, Edition 2
                      Frankfurt, Germany

The texts in this Student Textbook will refer you to the corresponding passages from these 4 books. Please also find an overview of these additional book readings on page 145.

The passages from these 4 books by Evangelist Reinhard Bonnke will provide you with profound biblical knowledge, with encouraging and challenging expertise, with enjoyable and uplifting testimonies of God's work in Evangelist Reinhard Bonnke's life, and with easy to understand and reality proven principles of effective soul-winning. Don't miss out on this extra blessing of inspiring and encouraging teaching.

We are convinced that this *Reinhard Bonnke School of Fire* study will sharpen your mind on soul-winning and will set you on fire to become a burning witness for Jesus Christ. You will experience for yourself that with God you can do "even greater things".

May God bless you and ignite you with a passion for the lost!
Thank you for taking part in the Great Commission of Jesus Christ.

Module I
Lesson 1: Basic Principles

Introduction by Evangelist Reinhard Bonnke

This introduction presents some essential truths that have stood me in good stead over the many years in which I have been involved in active evangelism. I pray that in this *School of Fire* study you will not merely gain "head knowledge" but be set afire by the flame which has lit the African continent in the great Gospel campaigns that it has been my unspeakable joy to lead.

I.1.1.   God's Word: the Manual of Faith

The Bible is God's burning bush. It is there that we encounter him and that he speaks. How we react is proof of who we are. This *School of Fire* study therefore also begins with the Bible.

I.1.1.1.   A Revelation of God

As a book, the Bible is in a class of its own, distinct from every other book ever written. It brings God into focus and brims over with his greatness. It is drama, the drama of time, a window through which we see God striding through the centuries with awesome power and majesty.

We must be clear about one thing: that the purpose of Scripture is to show us God and inspire our trust in him. The Bible is a manual of faith in God that has been given to us *"so that the man of God may be thoroughly equipped for every good work"* (2 Timothy 3:17). It is God's voice in the burning bush calling out to us as he called out to Moses

– urging us to surrender our questions and doubts, abandon our misgivings and go forward with him. The path will open up as we walk, just as the sea opened up before Moses.

Moses' encounter with God in the burning bush launched him on a vast, ridiculously impossible and hair-raising mission; armed with no more than a shepherd's crook he was pitted against the world's greatest military power. Hand in hand with the Lord, he set out on that daunting task and became the greatest name in the ancient world.

History, as recorded by human authors, naturally reflects their outlook on life. The Bible on the contrary is God's summary of events; it presents the divine view of things. It is utterly dependable; as Psalm 119:160 says, *"all* [God's] *words are true."* The Bible begins with an end and ends with a beginning, God ending the work of creation and beginning a new heaven and a new earth.

I.1.1.2.   A Call to Action

Scripture does not exist to make us think but to make us act. It is neither an academic treatise nor an encyclopedia full of explanations for anything and everything. It does not offer mere information to satisfy human curiosity, nor does it set out to crack riddles. The old rabbis argued for days about how many angels could dance on the point of a needle and unbelievers still invent "difficulties" about authors, authority, origins, inspiration and so on, but often only as an excuse to justify their own unbelief. The impression they convey is that they do not really want any answers, and ask the questions only to mask their attitude of heart. Faith is a torch. Switch it on and darkness is no problem!

My God is the God of the Bible, not the God of reason and tradition. God is love and reason cannot handle love. The central core of divine revelation is the atoning sacrifice of God's son, and only he himself knows what was in the depths of his consciousness and the mind of the Father as he hung on the cross. The revelation of God pivots on the hill called Calvary, which is where our focus should be. My own understanding rests squarely on the Bible as a whole, not on a random selection of snippets from it. The Bible presents a picture that is 4,500 years wide. I have spent my entire lifetime scanning it to try to gain a sense of its dimensions rather than just glimpse bits and pieces of it. Not every piece of the jigsaw puzzle is yet in place, but the picture is a lot clearer than it was when I first started out as a missionary nearly 40 years ago. Not everyone has the opportunities that it has been my privilege to enjoy but my aim in this *School of Fire* study is to allow thousands of others to benefit from the experience I have gained from the years spent in this divine gallery.

There are plenty of Bible critics but they have not produced any book that can hold a candle to the Bible's ability to handle the imponderable mysteries of life, and to bring us liberty and salvation. The books that they write are too clever by half. The Bible is the only book that unveils the face of God and allows us to see how God has revealed himself gradually over time as mankind was able to take it – *"rule on rule; a little here, a little there"* (Isaiah 28:10). We are now in the end times, when *"knowledge shall increase"*, as the angel told Daniel (Daniel 12:4 NKJV). Bible understanding has advanced tremendously over the last 50 years and the Word continues to shed new light daily. Yet one thing has not changed at all: that the Bible is the great and only answer to life's questions. There simply is no other.

Scripture is God-inspired to express God's concerns. What concerns him should concern us. The world is a continuous swirl of human events, thoughts and reactions that God has been watching for thousands of years. *"The Lord is on his heavenly throne. He observes the son of men; his eyes examine them"* (Psalm 11:4). We may be unaware of God's fatherly gaze but the Holy Spirit knows people and life's intricacies and how to touch the secret springs of human hearts – perhaps from oblique and surprising angles. To preach effectively, we must stand on the platform of the Word. Our divine instructions, like Timothy's, are to *"preach the Word"* (2 Timothy 4:2) – not a collection of commentaries on it!

Jesus said, *"My yoke is easy and my burden is light"* (Matthew 11:30); he has not given us boots of lead. Some people carry their faith about like a heavy burden, their knees buckling and their backs breaking under their scrupulous efforts to try to please God. Faith is meant to lift us up: *"They will soar on wings like eagles"* (Isaiah 40:31). I bear the responsibility for a worldwide work but find it a joy, a task that constantly demonstrates God's wonderful grace. It is a vision that the Lord has wonderfully enabled me to realize. In a thousand testing situations he has manifested encouragement to me and I relax. My prayer is that the lessons in this *School of Fire* study will help others to find the same assurance.

I.1.2.   Fire Power

I.1.2.1.   The Flame of Love

Two great revelations come to us through the Word: God is a consuming fire and God is love. They combine in a single flame of love. That image is central to an understanding of the Word and we cannot afford to neglect it.

God originally revealed himself to Moses as fire. It was a privileged moment in Moses' life but Moses did not go off and spend the rest of his life merely talking about his experience. God commissioned Moses for a specific task and the fire leaped from the bush into his heart. That day he started out on the most extraordinary career any man would ever know, changing the future of the whole world.

Whatever God reveals about himself is meant to have a practical impact on our lives, not simply to give us a topic of conversation. He does these things to put fire in our belly, not to give us an experience of euphoria, emotional satisfaction, or even blessings and thrills. Moses did not go back to the wilderness bush for a repeat experience. He went *from* there as God directed him. Then, 1,500 years later, on the day of Pentecost, the fire of God appeared again in Jerusalem where 120 disciples were sitting together in fellowship. It rested on each of them. Like Moses, they did not go back for a repeat experience. The fire had empowered them that day and they went out to do the job awaiting them.

I.1.2.2.   Offerings Made by Fire

God's touch torches us, makes firebrands of us and sets driftwood on fire. Students of a frozen professor of the Bible will be chips off the old iceberg and never warm anybody. The disciples said, *"Were not our hearts burning within us while he talked with us on the road?"* (Luke 24:32). Why were their hearts warmed? It was just that Jesus had explained the Scriptures to them about himself, bringing the old, familiar words to life. Their friends might have laughed at their feelings of delight, as unbelievers still do today. To the world such joy seems unnatural as the world has no experience that can compare with it and cannot understand people who are ablaze for the Lord. They are mocked as aliens, the primitive instinctive reaction that stems from ignorance and fear of what is strange and unknown. We know God and can smile.

Everything in this *School of Fire* study comes from the Bible and is about the Bible God of fire. Fire is his trademark: *"Fire goes before him"* (Psalm 97:3). If we are not "fired-up", we cannot convey God's nature to others. It may well be appropriate for a doctor to be clinical, cool and casual in his approach but for witnesses to the God of the burning bush, that will not do at all. The world is suffering from hypothermia. We need to go to the altar and tip its fire out onto the earth.

The first five books of the Bible, written by Moses, use the word "fire" over 160 times. All worship offerings, with the exception of the drink offering, were fire offerings. One phrase recurs like a major theme in the divine symphony: *"an offering made by fire"* (Leviticus 1:9). Clearly we were meant to remember that.

Writing to the Romans (12:1), Paul said, *"Offer your bodies* as *living sacrifices, holy and pleasing to God - this is your spiritual* [logical] *act of worship."* The combination of the Greek *somata*, meaning physical bodies, and *logiko* - from which we derive the English word "logical" - is significant; it points to the wholeness and harmony that God intended for our lives. The logic is that we cannot offer burnt sacrifices on a temple altar, so we have only ourselves to offer as living sacrifices. "Ourselves" means our love, strength, time and money. Today *we* are the *"offerings made by fire"* to the Lord.

I.1.2.3.   Fire Baptism

The last of the old covenant prophets was John the Baptist, *"a man who was sent from God"* (John 1:6) with the message *"Repent, for the kingdom of heaven is near"* (Matthew 3:2). When Israel had left Egypt, they passed through the Red Sea, the wilderness and the Jordan River. John wanted to recapitulate their beginnings, so he called them into the wilderness again to be baptized in the Jordan. His vision was of a re-born nation. He knew that water chilled but changed nobody and that baptism for repentance had no lasting effect. Then God told him about a new element - fire not water. Fire is the ultimate force of all change. Someone coming greater than John the Baptist would *"baptize with the Holy Spirit and with fire"* (Matthew 3:11) - and that baptism would be crucial.

Nicodemus, who was one of the leading members of the Sanhedrin, the supreme Jewish council, heard what John was proclaiming and recognized something of his own vision of a re-born nation, Israel as a kingdom of God. Nicodemus just had to find out more. So, under the cover of darkness, he went to visit Jesus and ask him some important questions. Jesus gave Nicodemus a full, if unexpected, answer. The whole nation was in a state of agitation because of Jesus' teachings. Jesus wasted no time and, going straight to the heart of the matter, he said, *"You must be born again"* (John 3:7). That "you" is plural, meaning the nation, not just Nicodemus; it was something for everyone. This important man did not immediately grasp what Jesus meant. He had hoped that John's baptism would achieve something but Jesus said, *"I tell you the truth, no one can enter the kingdom of God unless he is born of water and the Spirit"* (John 3:5). On the day of Pentecost Peter led 3,000 into salvation with similar words: *"Repent and be baptized. And you will receive the gift of the Holy Spirit"* (Acts 2:38). In other words, water and the Spirit were to be standard elements of the new life in Christ. And the Spirit was to be manifested as fire – as we will see.

When Peter saw Jesus raised from the dead, he certainly did not go straight out and preach about it. He could not believe his own eyes and was too apprehensive about how the authorities would react to the rumor of Jesus rising from the dead. The disciples gathered together to encourage each other because they lived in *"fear of the Jews"* (John 20:19). Peter did not know what to do but he had to do something so he decided to go fishing again, back to square one (John 21).

Then dawned the day of Pentecost and the fellowship meeting of the 120 disciples. The Holy Spirit came down to them through the heavens that had been torn apart by Christ's ascension and they were all filled with the Holy Spirit. *"They saw what seemed to be tongues of fire that separated and came to rest on each of them"* (Acts 2:3). They were transformed. That day they all stood up in public as witnesses of the resurrection (Acts 2:32). Peter preached and the crowds trembled at the power of his words.

The secret of their new-found boldness was the baptism in the Spirit and fire. They now knew – by their own experience – that Jesus had risen and had taken his place at the right hand of God. They became burning and shining lamps, witnesses to the resurrection. We never read again that they were silenced by threats or cowed by fear; instead, their life's work became to boldly declare the gospel wherever they went. *"God has not given us a spirit of fear, but of power and of love and of a sound mind"* (2 Timothy 1:7 NKJV).

There is no such thing as a cool God. His throne is not made of cold marble. If we are to know him, we must respond to his temperament of zeal, fire and love. The people whom God would describe as *"after my own heart"*, as he said of David (Acts 13:22), are not just decent and harmless members of society, but demonstrate vigor, valor and eagerness.

Whatever God tells us he is, that is what we need to know; God tells us what he wants us to be like when we are fire-baptized. We cannot be his representatives if we have a cold heart and frozen tongues; to do him justice we need tongues of fire. We also need a sense of his scale of operations, as we will now go on to see.

I.1.3.   Divine Dimensions

I.1.3.1.   God's Nature

After Moses had met the living God, he had everything still to learn about him. The day before the divine appearance in the desert, neither he nor anybody else knew anything, or very little, about God; they did not even know God's name. However, God immediately sent Moses out on that tremendous exodus venture and gave him the assurance that *"I am who I am"* (Exodus 3:14). Meeting God is all we need to get us going. Moses would find out who God was as he went along, seeing him at work – and that is our experience today. What God does is what he is; he never acts out of character. And the fundamental revelation is that God is fire.

Fire demonstrates God's nature but does not explain everything about him. Fire is far more than an outward show of God's glory or splendor. It displays his disposition, his infinite greatness, the central source of hope and life in the universe. Our best enthusiasm makes us no more than a smoldering wick alongside him, the eternal sun of righteousness. He is passionate in action. For example, three times in the Bible we read, *"The zeal of the Lord Almighty will accomplish this"* (2 Kings 19:31, Isaiah 9:7, Isaiah 37:32).

I.1.3.2.   Think Big!

That is God. To be his friends we must think big, think on a worldwide scale. The sector to which we are allocated may be small but the Lord puts us where he wants us and gives us allies greater than all the enemy, on the victory front. We are God's sons, commissioned ambassadors, demanding surrender to the King of kings.

The principal character in the Bible is God. The Book begins with the creation of heaven and earth, presenting God as a being with limitless power in a vast setting. In the first eleven chapters of Genesis the curtain is lifted on a global stage. Within a chapter or two it shows us how the awesome picture has degenerated into an awful scene of human guilt, carnage, violence and blood, the whole generation genetically corrupted. God in his heaven regretted that he had ever made man. So he took global action. His mighty hand turned on the fountains of the deep and opened the sluice gates of the sky in order to wash down the earth. The torrents of the Flood washed away bloodstain and pollution and removed the wicked from the face of the earth.

The Bible drama next shows God turning his attention away from the global scene to focus on one man, Abraham. God took him in hand and taught him the foundations of a better and righteous world order. The future did not lie in war and corruption. He spread before Abraham his plan to bless all families on earth, beginning with Abraham's own family. The Lord persisted with that family for long centuries, turbulent and rebellious as its members were, but his purpose never faltered for behind it lay the most powerful of all driving forces – love. *"I have loved you with an everlasting love; I have drawn you with loving kindness,"* he said (Jeremiah 31:3).

As the Bible story unfolds, it sweeps across the whole historic scene, the rise and fall of empires, Nineveh, Babylon, Assyria, Medes, Persia, Greece and then Rome. Nations squirmed under the iron heel of Rome's marching legions. Again God rose in majesty but he needed no military might. His answer was the baby born in a stable and placed in a cattle trough, with the voices of angel hosts singing in unison, performing the overture to the greatest drama of all eternity. On earth that drama culminated in the scene of a crucified Savior.

Then the divine camera once more panned the whole earth. Risen from the dead, Jesus sent his servants out on a global mission. They were not mighty warriors armed with sword and spear; they were nobodies, a random gathering of peasants and fishermen – with one major difference: they were Spirit and fire-baptized. *"Go into all the world and preach the good news to all creation,"* he told them (Mark 16:15). They went, crossing international borders, overturning ancient heathen cultures and carrying the flame of God into the dark, merciless and ancient order of cruelty and greed. The Book does not need to record what happened, for it was inevitable. The world caught the fire and pagan emperors bowed down to the Christian God. Today we are looking for another global act of God, the coming of Christ to reign as Lord of all lords.

Like Moses, we do not start out understanding God very well at all. Reading the Bible helps us there. The better we know him, the fewer our questions. Jesus said, *"In that day you will no longer ask me anything"* (John 16:23). We shall have no questions when we see him face to face. The process of getting to know him starts here: *"The fear of the Lord is the beginning of wisdom* (Proverbs 9:10). By the Word of God we know God, and appreciate his character and disposition. It reveals him, even if we see *"a poor reflection as in a mirror"*, but we can *"grow in the grace and knowledge of our Lord and Savior Jesus Christ"* (2 Peter 3:18). That was Peter's final word to us. The better we know God, the better we understand life.

I.1.4.   The Power of Love

I.1.4.1.   For God So Loved the World

The Word describes the passion of God. Salvation was formed in the furnace of God's heart for *"God so loved the world"* (John 3:16). God's love is a beacon on the hilltop of Calvary. The time came for Jesus to make his way to Jerusalem for the last time, by the Father's will, to the final act of redemption. The Gospels describe it. Jesus told the disciples he was going to Jerusalem where, he said, all prophets die. They were appalled at the danger. Thomas Didymus even said, *"Let us also go, that we may die with him"* (John 11:16). Brave words!

Mark 10:32 tells us: *"They were on their way up to Jerusalem, with Jesus leading the way, and the disciples were astonished, while those who followed were afraid."* They were astonished and afraid at his resolute step as he strode on, his body language telling the tale. He had talked about his "time" coming and this historic journey would end with his great prayer: *"Father, the time has come"* (John 17:1). He knew what that meant: *"For this I came into the world,"* he said. *"I have a baptism to undergo, and how distressed I am until it is completed!"* (John 18:37, Luke 12:50). It was a baptism of suffering. He passed through it to bring us his baptism of holy fire.

Those were hours that began changing the world, a fundamental transformation triggered by Jesus' plunging into the swirling waters of suffering, torture and death to save mankind. John, *"the disciple whom Jesus loved"* and who was perhaps the youngest of the apostolic band, stressed love more than anyone else whose writings are included in the Bible. Yet John made one thing abundantly clear: *"This is love: **not** that we loved God, but that he loved us and sent his Son as an atoning sacrifice for our sins"* (1 John 4:10). Our love for God is not even the same thing as his love for us. In Galilee and Jerusalem people had been staggered by Jesus' phenomenal compassion; prophets like Jeremiah and Hosea had spoken of something like that but it had never been seen until Jesus appeared in the streets.

Make no mistake about it, God's love for us is intensely passionate. If you look more closely at John 3:16, you will detect a wonderful subtlety. *"For God so loved the world ..."* it says. That *"so"* in Greek means "in that way", "thus", so that the phrase reads *"For God loved the world in that way ..."* What "that way" is we find in the previous two verses: *"Just as Moses lifted up the snake in the desert, so the Son of Man must be lifted up."* That is the way in which God loved us, by his Son becoming like a snake pinned to a pole. The snake is the symbol of sin, an image that runs throughout the Bible from Genesis 3 to Revelation 20. *"God made him who had no sin to be sin* (a snake) *for us"* (2 Corinthians 5:21). God loved the world like that – with *"his great love"*, as Paul put it (Ephesians 2:4). God's great love was his Son. He loved us with Christ crucified.

As we read on, we discover that *"God so loved the world* that *he gave his one and only son, that whoever believes in him shall not perish but have eternal life"*. The key words "so ... that" tell us clearly that God had planned a specific effect, a great contrivance of love. By that astounding scheme, with Christ becoming like Moses' snake, we have everlasting life.

I.1.4.2.   Christ's Redeeming Sacrifice

Our road must never diverge one inch away from that essential truth. The Calvary bypass leads nowhere. Faith in God is not just faith in the Almighty. It is faith in the Lamb of God. Faith has a double core, the death and resurrection of Christ. The lessons in this *School of Fire* study, whatever theology we set out, derive from Christ's passion and resurrection, the greatest divine episode of all, the greatest thing even God ever did.

Revelation 5 lifts the curtain on the great scene of praise in which the Lamb occupies all heaven, all thought and all utterance. That is the focus of our praise today – the Lamb of God that takes away the sin of the world. We do not worship God to acquire power, because we like the music, to obtain his blessing, to generate miracles, or, in fact, to get anything at all. Actually, we gain a lot because to draw near in heart to God is to come to the life-centre of all blessing and all joy.

We praise God because we have those things already: *"Praise be to the God and Father of our Lord Jesus Christ, who has blessed us in the heavenly realms with every spiritual blessing in Christ"* (Ephesians 1:3). Our praise is love-praise, pure adoration of him. We thank him for power and the privilege of serving him.

Many cannot see the glory of Christ's redeeming sacrifice. Certainly, its depths are unfathomable. Calvary is the outworking of the love of God in the harsh language of sweat, blood, tears and death. Only God knows what that is like. Mortals can only stand and look on at the experience of an infinite God. The Cross illustrates far more than we have the capacity to appreciate. The reality is incomprehensible. Proverbs 14:10 says, *"Each heart knows its own bitterness, and no one else can share its joy."* That is a thousand times truer with the heart of God. That ghastly scene on the dark and awful Friday afternoon of the Jewish Passover – that is God, with the flame of love burning brightly.

I.1.4.3.   Fire Coupled with Love

A week before his crucifixion, Jesus went into the Temple courts. Worshippers had to buy their approved offerings there and exchange their secular Roman money for Temple shekels. The profiteers were exploiting the worshippers ruthlessly. Jesus did not mince his words or resort to British understatement: he called them robbers (Luke 19:46). Divine wrath rose up in this meek and lowly Jesus. He cleared the whole market. At the sight of him, a towering figure of righteous anger, everybody fled. It will happen again when he comes back and the unrighteous call, *"Hide us from the face of him who sits on the throne and from the wrath of the Lamb"* (Revelation 6:16). An angry Lamb! That is God.

A text came into the minds of the disciples as they saw Jesus' reaction to what was going on in the Temple courts: *"Zeal for your house will consume me"* (John 2:17, Psalm 69:9). Jesus fulfilled Malachi's prophesy as well as that of John the Baptist: *"Suddenly the Lord you are seeking will come to his temple. But who can endure the day of his coming? For he will be like a refiner's fire"* (Malachi 3:1-2).

Paul reminded Porcius Festus, the procurator of Judea, that the
events of Christ's death and resurrection were *"not done in a corner"*
(Acts 26:26). Festus judged Paul innocent but failed to release him,
just as Pilate failed to release Jesus. However, the death of Jesus was
to affect more than Jerusalem. God's love is for the whole world. He is
the God of the whole earth, not just the God of the Temple, cathedrals
or back street mission halls. When we open the New Testament, big
things immediately come into view. This carpenter from Nazareth,
dying like any wretched murderer, talked of his gospel permeating
the whole world. We have his global commission and his Kingdom
will not cease to expand (Isaiah 9:7).

The ancient prophets were often men of doom and people probably
hoped that what they predicted would not come true. God said,
"All the people on the face of the earth will tremble at my presence"
(Ezekiel 38:20). The prophet Haggai heard God say, *"I will shake
all nations. I will shake the heavens and the earth"* (Haggai 2:7,21).
*"I will make the heavens tremble; and the earth will shake from its place
at the wrath of the Lord Almighty, in the day of his burning anger"*
(Isaiah 13:13). That does not sound like a fun time! However, the
prophecies will come about and earth and heaven will be shaken.
The difference is that that same earth-shaking might is exercised in
mercy, fire coupled with love. Fire devours the enemies of mankind
out of love for his creation. Heaven has already been shaken when its
gates opened and the Lord passed through to Bethlehem. Then from
Bethlehem, where he lived, he went out to pass through the shade
of the olive trees in Gethsemane and to pray until his sweat turned
to blood and his anguish was overwhelming as he battled with the
forces of cosmic evil.

I have held this familiar picture up again to remind ourselves that
the kind of God we proclaim and work for is not a fancy ideal but the
God who is at one and the same time the God of the burning bush that
shook Egypt and the God who weeps and agonizes over lost people,
the one with wounded feet who goes searching for them to the far
flung corners of his dominion. Anyone who wants to be an evangelist
needs to know that this is our God.

Module I
Lesson 2: Basic Principles (continued)

Introduction by Evangelist Reinhard Bonnke

I.2.1. Word of Fire

This *School of Fire* study contains a great deal of information, particularly about Scripture and the work of God. That is vital. Those truths have been quarried from the depths of Scripture over the centuries like coal, "black diamonds" being brought to the surface from the depths of the mine. Black and cold, coal may lie in a heap or bunker like so much rubble. But when it is lit in the fireplace, it burns, bringing warmth and comfort and power. Our Bible knowledge, our theology must also be set alight so that it can warm the heart of the world. *"Is not my word like a fire?"* (Jeremiah 23:29).

I.2.1.1. Knowing God's Word

In New Testament times those who knew Scripture better than anyone else were the scribes and doctors of the law. Handling it daily, they believed, would earn them favor with God, enough to save them. To them the Bible was so sacred that it had intrinsic power, a kind of magic. They tried to trap Jesus with tricky Bible problems. On one occasion they confronted him with a made-up conundrum but his reply shocked them: *"You are in error because you do not know the Scriptures or the power of God"* (Matthew 22:29). They could not believe their ears! They, the Bible experts, did not know the Scriptures? Why, they could recite entire books by heart! However, as we said right at the beginning of this introduction, there are ways of knowing that have little to do with intellectual prowess. That is exactly the point that Jesus was making here; they had no knowledge of God's power and therefore they did not "know" the Scriptures.

That is the crux of the matter. We only really know the Scriptures to
the extent of our experience of God's power. The Word must be alive
in us if we are to really "know" it. The gospel is not words; *"it is the
power of God for the salvation of everyone who believes"* (Romans 1:16).
If we do not believe, its power remains inactive – and that is not what
God intended. *"The Word of God is living and active"* (Hebrew 4:12).

I.2.2.   Relaying the Fire

I.2.2.1.   Faith

If we are to be successful evangelists, we need to ask an important
question: how does Bible knowledge catch fire? Well, how does coal
catch fire? It is a combustible substance, meaning that we can easily
get it to burn, releasing warmth and energy. Our Bible knowledge
also can bring warmth and energy. We fan it to flame by our faith.
Faith alone releases the power of the Word of God. Faith itself is not a
mighty explosive force. It is intangible, not quantifiable, having neither size, shape, nor weight. Jesus said it was like a mustard seed. The
Word of God is highly inflammable and one tiny spark of faith is all
that is needed to set it ablaze. A spark can cause an explosion.

Paul said that Israel's privilege of hearing the Word of God was of no
value to them (Hebrew 4:2) because they did not mix it with faith.
The message was combustible but not activated; its potential could
have changed the nation but it was never realized. Israel's failing is
a warning to us. Theology, learning and erudition are nothing until
there is a day of Pentecost.

I.2.2.2.   Baptism in the Holy Spirit

In the beginning, at creation, the Holy Spirit did nothing, hovering
about and waiting. When the Word was spoken, the Holy Spirit

responded and created heaven and earth. That is the divine order – the Spirit waits for the Word and the Word needs the Spirit.

There are various ways to describe the Spirit in our lives. John the Baptist said Christ would *"baptize"* us in the Holy Spirit. "Baptize" has now become a purely religious term but originally it was a word used in commercial circles for dipping or soaking cloth in dye. The "baptized" material took on the nature of the element into which it was dipped; it absorbed its color. The cloth was in the dye and the dye in the cloth. To be baptized in the Spirit means that we are in the Spirit and the Spirit in us; we take on the character of the Spirit. We do not try to achieve it; it is what happens in baptism.

Absorbing the nature of the Spirit produces what Paul calls the *"fruit of the Spirit"* – love, joy, peace, patience, kindness, goodness, faithfulness, gentleness and self-control (Galatians 5:22-23). These virtues develop in our character and disposition as we allow the Spirit to operate.

I.2.2.3.   Living in the Holy Spirit

We must practice living as Spirit-filled children of God – live in the Spirit, pray in the Spirit, walk in the Spirit, or, if you like, swim in the waters of the Spirit flowing from the throne. Some are only paddling or wading in the shallows, but others have found the waters to swim in that Ezekiel described. Whether portrayed as water or fire, the Holy Spirit is essential.

Living in the Spirit does not mean a life of labor and perfectionism, inventing ways of self-denial to gain credit with God. Self-denial may be necessary in our service for God, but sacrifice for the sake of sacrifice is not a means of grace. That has been the error of all ascetics. Some early Christians were determined to be martyrs – but most people find that kind of lifestyle decidedly unappealing. We are not supposed to witness to a death wish. Neither are we supposed to suggest that we have to struggle to be people of the Spirit, worrying about it daily. Perhaps we want to be known as a man of prayer or a woman of the Spirit. That is Pharisaic. As I have already pointed out, Christ said, *"My yoke is easy and my burden is light"* (Matthew 11:30). He would know, for as a carpenter he once made yokes. His yokes did not chafe oxen, nor do they chafe us. And most people can cope with that.

It is absurd to be anxiously watching every moment exhausting ourselves trying to be Spirit-filled. The promise is that *"the joy of the Lord is your strength"* (Nehemiah 8:10). Living in the Spirit we walk with God with a confident bearing, live more easily, and pray more easily. *"Keep in step with the Spirit"* is the advice found in Galatians 5:25. Remember, the Holy Spirit is a gift, not a goal.

I.2.3.   The Undying Flame

I.2.3.1.   Holy Spirit Fire

The central altar of Israel had been lit by fire from heaven (2 Chronicle 7:1). To re-light the altar by any other means was to use false fire (Numeri 3:4). In fact, the fire was never to go out: *"The fire must be kept burning on the altar continuously; it must not go out"* (Leviticus 6:13). The anointed priests had to tend the sacred altar flame night and day. Their task was to clean up the ashes! The perpetual altar flame was a symbol not of what we have to do but of what God does. His fire never flickers or dies. The priests did not light a new fire every day, and the Lord does not need to re-light his fire on the altar of our heart daily.

Someone walking through the peat bogs of Ireland may see the will-o'-the-wisp flame flitting ahead of them but it cannot be captured. I get the impression that some people think of the Holy Spirit fire like that – always there but always out of reach. It is amazing how some despair and labor for the Spirit, whereas if there is one thing that is absolutely necessary and absolutely promised, it is that if we ask for the Spirit, we will receive him (Luke 11:9-13).

Another important thing we need to understand is the indivisible oneness of the Holy Spirit. Before God's throne John saw seven lamps burning which he said were the seven spirits of God (Revelation 4:5). The same seven spirits are spoken of in Revelation 1:4 and 5:6. Looking closer, we see something very special about those seven lamps: they derive their energy from one source, one Spirit. His flame can be divided into seven, or into 120 as on the day of Pentecost, but he is still *"one Spirit"* (1 Corinthians 12:4).

The Spirit comes to us himself. We do not receive some of him or need a topping-up from time to time. Scripture never talks about *some* Holy Spirit or *more* Holy Spirit. On the day of Pentecost each person received the Holy Spirit – not just a little bit of him. He is the third Person of the Trinity – beyond personality, in fact – and he is the one we are given. Similarly, we are promised Christ's presence wherever we meet in his name. He is there – not just a foot or finger but, by his infinite omnipresence, his full being.

The reference to seven heavenly lamps relates to the seven-branched lamp stand lighting up the Holy Place of the Jerusalem Temple, the menorah. The same reference is found in Zechariah 4, one of the many Old Testament allusions in Revelation. The prophet Zechariah had a strange vision of a lamp stand with seven branches fed by seven pipes from the bowl of olive oil on the top. His vision held a secret – how the lamps never went out and the bowl of oil was always full. Zechariah was shown the secret. Two olive trees fed the bowl with oil from a constantly renewable source.

I.2.3.2.   The Eternal Spirit

That reminds us of the never-ending supply of oil with which God rewarded a widow of Zarephath who sacrificed her last food for Elijah the prophet (1 Kings 17:7-16). That is what the Spirit is like, endlessly new. He is the *"eternal Spirit"* (Hebrew 9:14). God is always on full strength, never a waning force, always saying *"I am!"* He is *"the Father of the heavenly lights, who does not change by shifting shadows"*

(James 1:17). Our experience of the Spirit would be uncharacteristic if it proved volatile, vaporizing, or began to fade like a battery in a torch. The Holy Spirit does not flit about like a startled bird, here today and gone tomorrow.

The Old Testament anointing was with oil but as a symbol of the oil of the Spirit. Until the day of Pentecost, the Holy Spirit *"had not been given"* (John 7:39). He had appeared only briefly in Old Testament times to empower a man or woman for a special occasion. Jesus' promise was that the Spirit would be our constant companion. He said, *"I will ask the Father, and he will give you another Counselor to be with you for ever"* (John 14:16). That Counselor, the eternal Spirit, does not gradually die out in our lives. We do not receive some Spirit, for a limited time. *"From the fullness of his grace we have all received one blessing after another"* (John 1:16). Fullness is the name of what we receive.

I.2.3.3.   The Anointing

The coming of the Holy Spirit is the anointing. *"God anointed Jesus of Nazareth with the Holy Spirit and power"* (Acts 10:38). In Luke 4:18 Jesus quoted Isaiah: *"The Spirit of the Lord is on me, because he has anointed me."* The anointing gave Israel's kings authority. They were anointed only once and the anointing was permanent. *"You have an anointing from the Holy One ... the anointing you received from him remains in you"* (1 John 2:20,27).

We receive the Spirit from Christ as the promise of the Father. We do not receive it from anybody else. The commission is transferable but not the anointing. We do not go for a second-hand anointing. What we have is designed for each of us. We may pray for others but we have no authority to give the Spirit – it is a personal gift from God.

It is important, however, for us to remain in him. In John 15:1-8 Jesus described himself as the vine and disciples as fruit-bearing branches. He warned us: *"Apart from me you can do nothing"* (John 15:5). As long as we remain in him there is no pause in the flow of life. *"The trees of the Lord are well watered"* (Psalm 104:16). It is a permanent necessity, not an intermittent benefit reserved for special prayer meetings.

I need to point out that we may not have a physical sensation of God's abiding fullness every day. God is a Spirit. A strong man does not feel a current of strength when he is sitting; he feels no different to any other man. He revels in his strength when he exercises it. There certainly are times when we are very conscious of the presence and power of the Holy Spirit, but he is present with us at all other times. Personally, I have felt healing power in my hands only once but I have seen God working amazing marvels time and time again. In fact, I even heard of a miracle taking place as I was preparing these words. This very day a paraplegic in a wheelchair, a member of the paraplegic sports group, was restored to perfect mobility and walking and running while I was ministering.

Our need of the constant anointing is crucial to God's scheme. We are anointed to do his work and win the world by our Holy Spirit witness. There must be no uncertainty. The destiny of generations rests upon it. If the Holy Spirit fluttered away and the power of the Spirit faded, our witness would fade and the salvation of lost people would be in jeopardy. God cannot afford to leave it to us to arrange fullness by labor and prayer. The witness must go on. The Spirit does not go away, although things appeared to have been different in Old Testament times; David prayed, *"Do not take your Holy Spirit from me"* (Psalm 51:11). However, when Christ ascended to heaven, he gave us the Spirit for ever, as we have already pointed out.

Never once after the day of Pentecost did anyone pray for another anointing. Nowhere are we told to pray for power after we receive the anointing Spirit. The river flows on; the water does not spurt out spasmodically. The theory of "many fillings" or many anointings is totally foreign to New Testament teaching and has been imported from opponents of Spirit-filled testimony. David had only one anointing of God. Saul was anointed. He failed God which cost his life in battle but David still called him *"the Lord's anointed"* (1 Samuel 24:6).

I.2.3.4.   The Abiding Spirit

It is sad to find believers uncertain of God's power and the presence of his Spirit. They expend a lot of effort in prayer and in introspection as if the Holy Spirit were a hard-won prize. This makes nobody sure whether they are full of Spirit or not. One ridiculous idea is that power is proportionate to time spent in prayer, two hours bringing twice as much as one hour. That is a human concept, not Scripture. The New Testament has 200 references to prayer and its importance but nothing about praying for power. The fact is that the promise of the abiding Spirit is just too big for some people's faith. God is with us and we must believe it as we go out in his name to face a hostile world.

Jesus did not specify hyper-spirituality as a qualification for receiving the Spirit. Jesus said, *"Ask and it will be given to you. Everyone who asks receives"* (Matthew 7:7-8). Receiving the Holy Spirit is not conditional on good behavior. The Holy Spirit is the unmerited gift of God (see Galatians 3:2). That is all and it is happening everywhere, to hundreds of people daily. This is the undying Pentecostal tongue of flame. We may grieve the Spirit, or quench the Spirit, but only if he is with us to be grieved or quenched. The gift of the Holy Spirit is God's commitment to us.

A colleague told me of a church where the Holy Spirit burst in on a meeting, so they arranged further meetings to enjoy more of the same blessing. The first meeting got under way and nothing happened – or rather nothing happened that they had expected. After a few attempts and disappointments, they gave up. For years afterwards they blamed it on each another, digging up all sorts of supposed faults and spiritual failures. Their pastor had misled the church into believing that the measure of their perfection was the measure of God's blessing, like a reward for good behavior. The truth that gives us the freedom of God is that there is no such formula!

We are used to power cuts. All the forces we know diminish and need renewal. Evaporation takes place, our strength drains away and the car battery goes flat. That is the law of nature, entropy. Yet there is, and has to be, a non-diminishing source, and that source is the power of God. That same undying energy is given to believers as the gift of eternal life. Our own physical strength may fail, but even in our declining years God's Spirit within us remains active. *"The righteous will flourish like a palm tree, they will grow like a cedar of Lebanon ... they will still bear fruit in old age, they will stay fresh and green"* (Psalm 92:12-14).

The laws of thermodynamics state that as the energies of the universe change a loss occurs and finally the whole cosmos will die. God is different – he does not change and neither does his Spirit. God began all things. His power is eternal and never diminishes, and that is the life he has given us in our salvation.

I.2.4. Divine Goodness

I.2.4.1. Compelled by the Love of Christ

The Bible is not a mere handbook of miracles. Christianity is not just about how to "get things". The foundation of faith has to do with the redeeming work of Christ. Our work must relate to it. Work is worship. Worship is more than what you do in church – that is only the 'cult' expression of it. Worship is our trust in God for and in our daily lives. We do not worship God to create an atmosphere or to get miracles. Our reason is love; we come to him, enjoy his presence. To worship him without the desire for his presence is a cold business.

Again we see that what God says is intended to have an effect on our lives, to be reflected in our personality as well as in our work, witness and evangelism. God's love is for the world – not the world system which is evil, or the material world, but the people. That is his call to us, to stand by his side in active life loving the world, and, if it comes to it and is necessary, we may *"fill up in [our] flesh what is still lacking in regard to Christ's afflictions, for the sake of his body, which is the church"* (Colossians 1:24). Church expansion can be merely a business enterprise carried out on business lines. Growth, filling church pews, is not our motive; it is as Paul said, *"Christ's love compels us"* (2 Corinthians 5:14).

When disaster falls, everyone asks why God did not prevent it. They assume that he could. Most people know instinctively that God has the ability to work miracles. God is, by definition, the Almighty but most of us would like to tell God what he should do, as if we were wiser or kinder than he is. If people do not get the miracle they want, they decide they do not believe in miracles. I think we can almost feel sorry for God as he has to face the barriers we put up!

When Moses first met God in the brilliance of that blazing bush, he had little understanding. He fell on his face in fear because he had seen God. He saw God's power unleashed against the Egyptian empire, and at Sinai, and knew him as a great and dreadful God. Daniel called him *"the great and awesome God"* (Daniel 9:4). But as Moses approached the end of his life, he had drawn closer to God than when he first met him at the burning bush.

I.2.4.2.   The God of Favor

Moses prophesied about the tribes of Israel, one by one. About Joseph, the father of two tribes, Manasseh and Ephraim, he said: *"May the Lord bless his land with the best gifts of the earth and its fullness and the favor of him who dwelt in the burning bush"* (Deuteronomy 33:13). That lovely expression, *"the favor of him who dwelt in the burning bush"*, describes the Lord, and we see it in the face of Jesus. Moses was the agent of omnipotence to make Egypt tremble with plagues, desolation and even death, but behind such a display was the God of "favor." God does not will the death of any sinner; he is slow to get angry and quick to forgive. The apostle Paul's spoke about the will of God: *"You will be able to test and approve what God's will is – his good, pleasing and perfect will"* (Romans 12:2).

God is good. What does that mean? What is his idea of goodness? Well, we can see that from the beginning: *"God saw all that he had made, and it was very good"* (Genesis 1:31). His ideas of goodness are like ours, the richness of life. Indeed, where else would we get our ideas from? He came to Abraham who had not prayed and God said, *"I will bless you and all peoples on earth will be blessed through you"* (Genesis 12:2-3). We are told what that meant: *"Abram had become very wealthy in livestock and in silver and gold"* (Genesis 13:1). At the end of his life we read: *"Abraham was now old and the Lord has blessed him* in every way" (Genesis 24:1). God's blessing is tangible, practical and real.

God's will is not trouble, sickness or misfortune. Such things are never called "good"' in Scripture and God does not send them. They are oppression. That does not mean we are immune to them; they are part of life in an imperfect world. In fact, God has put us here on earth knowing that we will be exposed to stress and strain. To his glory we are to prove his grace and strength to endure and overcome. They are his tests, preparing us for his eternal plans.

One of the worst human trials is illness. So it becomes a specific interest of God, as we see in the work of Jesus. We are told: *"Pray one for each other so that you may be healed"* (James 5:16). Sickness is a stubborn enemy as it arises from the fall of man. Not every sickness is healed - for many reasons. But whether it is healed or not, our prayers are important and every prayer is heard - God is never deaf.

When we pray for good things, we need to remember that *"every good and perfect gift is from above, coming down from the Father of the heavenly lights"* (James 1:17). The father of lights is the sun ceaselessly pouring out light and warmth as the means of fertility and richness of this planet; that is how God pours out his goodness unceasingly as the God of love and creation. God's will is good, good in human terms, but his will is certainly not being done on earth, very far from it. Jesus taught us to pray, *"Your will be done"* (Matthew 6:10).

I.2.5.   Practical Advice

1. Burn for God!

The burning bush burned on and was not consumed. That is our role – we burn on and we are not consumed. God wants us to keep on burning, not burn out. He has no use for cinders. Some are consumed by lust, the love of money or power, and it destroys them. They become soulless, empty shells. Some individuals spend their lives dissatisfied; grumbling until grumbling is all that is left of them. They end up as a grumble. The love of God has no parallel with that. It builds up, enriches us and is ultimately the making of us.

2. Take Action!

We all pray "Lord, use me!" If we are useable, we will be used automatically, but we are living people, not inanimate tools, or pots. I have been asked: "Why doesn't God use some people when they ask?" God does not "use" them because all they ever do is ask. They are not useable because they do nothing but wait to be used. God uses only animate people, not empty pots waiting to be picked up. God acts with those who act, works with workers, not "waiters."

3. Live the Word!

Make the Word of God your book. Read it! *"Let the Word of Christ dwell in you richly"* (Colossians 3:16). Preach the Word and live the engrafted Word, for God blesses his Word. Have faith in God and the Word will ignite and warm your soul.

Module I
Lesson 3:
Salvation as a Doctrine and Experience

Reference: *Time Is Running Out*

I.3.1.   The Biblical Theology of Salvation

It is the desire of God that all should be saved. Salvation is the means
whereby a righteous God makes an unrighteous people acceptable
and clean in his sight and presence. Were it not for God's redemptive
sacrifice through Jesus Christ, the sins of mankind would end only
in destruction, with no hope of escape from the punishment those
sins deserve. Through salvation, God offers the riches of his grace,
the bounty of his Kingdom, and the assurance of eternal life. None of
these will ever be attained by the frail efforts of a fallen world. Man
cannot save himself. He has neither the capabilities nor the right to do
so. Salvation comes from God to man; it is not initiated nor controlled
by the whims of man himself.

If salvation were attainable through the efforts of mankind,
Ephesians 2:8-9 would be meaningless. The crucifixion of Jesus Christ
would be a horrible wasted effort on the part of God's son. His death
would be unnecessary. If man could save himself, the promise of
John 3:16 would be irrelevant. There would be no need for a son to be
sacrificed and belief on that son would be inconsequential.

I.3.1.1.   The Fall of Humanity

God's plan for his creation is evident through the biblical account
of Adam and Eve in the Garden of Eden (Genesis 2). Mankind was
given dominion over the earth and the relationship between God,

mankind and the rest of creation was ordered and perfect, within the boundaries established by the Creator. But God did not want robotic slaves who simply responded to him because of predetermined and controlled response mechanisms. He also gave mankind the freedom to make decisions, a free will to choose, or not choose, how to live and how to serve the Creator.

Mankind wasn't satisfied with that. Through willful violation of God's laws (Genesis 3), the bonds of those relationships were broken and sin and its consequences were embraced. Sin, disobedience, rebellion brought death and destruction to the world. By free choice, mankind chose to separate himself from the Creator. This was not God's plan. It was a result of satanic influence preying upon the ego of a humanity that could not look beyond its own selfish desires. This is not the relationship God wanted with his creation.

As a result, since that time, mankind's attempts to reconcile himself to his creator have been ineffective and inadequate. No sacrifice, great or small, has been sufficient to make full restitution for the sin debt owed by mankind. Only through the grace of God's redemption has it been possible for mankind to again enjoy the unity with God that was part of the Creator's divine plan. Even that, however, is less than what was originally designed because of the limitations of creation. Though the sin may be forgiven, the consequences of that sin remain and the influence of evil is still strongly felt in the world today.

What are the consequences of sin, the consequences of the "lost" nature of mankind? Everyday we are bombarded with tales of horror and depravity which demonstrate the lowliness of the "lost" nature of man. Separation from the impact of God's redemptive glory has resulted in a society in which sin and evil, in most respects, are considered the norm and righteousness is looked upon with disdain. Wallowing in its own sin nature, mankind seeks its self-preservation, self-indulgence and self-gratification at the expense and loss of others. At best, relationships are fragile and easily broken. Addictions and bondages of every sort are rampant as mankind attempts to cover up the ravages of sin's guilt. The world looks for human relief from sickness and explains away the impact of poverty and crime as something to be addressed totally from a social perspective, with no recognition of the effects of sin in a godless society. Satan wants nothing less than to convince the world that each individual is of greater importance than others and there is no action too repugnant to sway mankind from its course of self-promotion and self-fulfillment. "People suffer chiefly for one reason: They have chosen to ignore God's rule book, the Bible, and everything has gone terribly wrong as a result." (*Time Is Running Out*)

The cry of a lost humanity and the need for salvation are ignored and unrecognized. The gospel of Christ is either white-washed or not presented at all, lest it offend. Mankind doesn't even recognize its need for a savior. As Evangelist Bonnke writes, "the devil schemes to hide this obvious fact from us. His policies of murder and genocide having failed to prevent the birth of our Savior (see Matthew 2:16-18) and later, His resurrection, the only other alternative of Satan [is] to prevent the preaching of the gospel." (*Time Is Running Out*)

Additional Reading

Read from *Time Is Running Out*
"The Fall and Rise of Man" on pages 29-32
of the book passage compilation

I.3.1.2. Humanity's Need for a Savior

Through the acts of sinful humanity (Galatians 5:19-21), social order and morality have deteriorated to a level far below even the depravity of ancient Rome. Mankind, in its attempt to restore the essence of order and morality, has sought (and continues to search) for any means that will create feelings of goodness while not infringing upon the rights and values of others. Substitutions for the gospel have developed in an attempt to soothe the cry for healing and restoration.

Self-help and "feel good" messages are strongly touted as the panacea for everything that is wrong in the world.

Recognizing the need for resolution, all the while refusing to accept the need for a savior, humanity seeks to rectify the ills of society by establishing substitute religions, emphasizing the importance of good works and promoting the values of a humanistic world perspective. The essence of these views, however, is vanity; such cries of humanity are meaningless (Ecclesiastes 12:8). The efforts of mankind alone cannot bring reconciliation. Quite the contrary, man's sinful nature fights against reconciliation through coercion and deceit, compelling all to accept politically correct resolutions that are effete, ineffective and inadequate. Mankind rationalizes away the truth of the gospel by promoting acceptance of all views and denigrating gospel truth as prejudicial and offensive.

"Today the problem of spirituality is being tackled in various ways by people of different beliefs and backgrounds. For example, some try to reconcile themselves and their beliefs to the gospel by claiming that Christianity is not unique, but in essence the same as all religions; that it is just a matter of common experience." (*Time Is Running Out*)

The Bible clearly states that everyone is a sinner (Romans 3:23) and that salvation comes only through Jesus Christ (John 14:6). That's the gospel. If we accept the gospel as truth, then we cannot, dare not, compromise that truth out of fear of offending. If we deny the gospel, then we deny the very Christ who died for our sins and reject the knowledge that salvation comes through him, and him only. Jesus said, "whosoever shall deny me before men, him will I also deny before my Father which is in heaven" (Matthew 10:33) [See also 2 Timothy 2:12].

Humanity does not accept the universality of sin and the implications and nature of "lostness." Those who recognize their own sinfulness are ridiculed as ignorant and unenlightened, suffering rejection at the very hands of those who so loudly cry that all views are to be accepted and embraced. Humanity fails to grasp the inconsistencies of its own proclamations of universal acceptance of all while persecuting any whose beliefs are contrary to what is considered accepted norm.

If all views are acceptable (as modern society would dictate), why is Christianity chastised so strongly by those who claim to be enlightened? Quite simply, when confronted with the reality of sin, mankind must either repent or reject. If mankind repents, he must face his own sinfulness and accept the consequences of his sin. Repentance brings salvation. On the other hand, if mankind rejects the reality of sin, he must also fight to destroy those who remind him of the depravity of his sinful nature. In so doing, he deludes himself into believing that his sin is nonexistent and those who reveal the sin are the ones who are wrong.

Additional Reading

**Read from *Time Is Running Out*
chapter 14 on pages 40-53 of the book passage compilation
and *Reflections of Reality* on page 7 of the book passage compilation**

Module I
Lesson 4:

Salvation as a Doctrine and Experience
(continued)

References: *Time Is Running Out* and *Faith - The Link With God's Power*

I.4.1.   The Biblical Theology of Salvation (continued)

I.4.1.1.   God's Promise

Humanity's sin destroyed the relationship it shared with its creator.
No effort of man was sufficient to repair the damage and bridge
the chasm that separated mankind from God. Man's attempts were
powerless and inadequate. Nevertheless, God, in his love for his
creation, looked beyond the impact and disgrace of sin and promised
a means whereby mankind could once again be reconciled in its
relationship with the Father. That move of God toward reconciliation
began even while the stain of Adam and Eve's sin was still fresh. God
promised a redeemer who would bring mankind back into a right
relationship with himself.

In Eden, the promise was a "seed" that would bruise the head of
the serpent (Genesis 3). In the prophets, the promise was a messiah,
descended from the throne of David. (Isaiah 11) In the New Testament,
the promise was proclaimed by John the Baptist as one who would
come after him, bringing grace, peace and forgiveness (John 1).

As mankind sought to fulfill its own redemption, it moved itself
farther and farther away from God. Only a perfect offering could
amend for sin; only a perfect sacrifice could reinstate mankind to its
original place within the kingdom of God.

The sacrificial system established by God through the children of Israel was only a temporary means of atonement (Leviticus 4ff,16). It was inadequate to make full recompense for the guilt of sin. Throughout Israel's history, the prophets foretold of the coming of a messiah to provide the ultimate propitiation for sin, one who would, once and for all, bridge the chasm of sin that had separated man from God.

Additional Reading

Read from *Time Is Running Out*
chapter 3 on pages 10-14 of the book passage compilation

I.4.1.2.   The Promise Fulfilled

"But when the time had fully come, God sent his Son born of a woman, born under law, to redeem those under law, that we might receive the full rights of sons." (Galatians 4:4-5, NIV)

The promised redemption was fulfilled through the birth, death and resurrection of Jesus Christ. He became the sacrifice to make recompense for the sins of mankind. Through his life and ministry he continually questioned the laws and rituals of the day, declaring them inadequate to make reconciliation to God; he drove the moneychangers out of the Temple, rejecting the legalism of the ritualism of the day; he referred to the Pharisees as hypocrites, wallowing in self pride; and he proclaimed that real salvation and service to God comes from the heart and is not dictated by the laws of man, challenging the religious hypocrisy of the day. He was not the savior the religious leaders were looking for; he was the savior the people needed.

Satan tried to stop him, but to no avail. He failed to prevent the Savior's birth (Matthew 2:16-18). Satan's apparent triumph at the crucifixion was crushed by the resurrection (Mark 16:6-7).

His persecution of the early church only made the church stronger and more resolute in its efforts to fulfill its commission to spread the gospel (Acts 1:8).

The hope of the church today is the promised return of Christ (1 Thessalonians 4:16-17). Until that time, however, the great commission (Matthew 28:19-20) still remains as the duty of all believers.

Additional Reading

Read from *Time Is Running Out*
***The Second Coming* on pages 8-9 and**
***Back to the Great Commission* on pages 15-16**
of the book passage compilation

I.4.1.3.   Faith

When asked to define faith, many Christians simply quote Hebrews 11:1 (*"Now faith is the substance of things hoped for, the evidence of things not seen."*) without a clear understanding of what faith really is and its importance to believers today. Evangelist Bonnke states that following Jesus requires faith. Without faith, it is impossible to do so. For the evangelist to be effective in ministry, he must have faith himself and then must pass that faith on to those being evangelized. That is, faith has to first be caught before it can be taught. (*Time Is Running Out*)

What, then, is faith? What is its nature and why is it important? "Faith is a personal relationship, not a mathematical relationship between numbers. Faith is the eye to see the unseen." It is a "kind of immune system filtering out fears that otherwise would paralyze all activity." (*Faith - The Link With God's Power*)

Consider again Ephesians 2:8-9 (NIV). *"For it is by grace you have been saved, through faith - and this not from yourselves, it is the gift of God - not by works, so that no one can boast."* Salvation is not based on the works, efforts or achievements of mankind. If achievements were the means whereby salvation could be attained, only those who have certain levels of success would be worthy to be saved. Who would establish the standards to determine worthiness? How would one know if he had done enough, achieved enough, to merit God's love and forgiveness?

That's where faith becomes so important. It does not matter what success level or achievement level an individual attains. In a world where an individual's worth or esteem is often wrongfully measured by financial success or celebrity status, it is difficult to fathom that God does not have similar requirements that must be met in order for salvation to be granted. In actuality, he does have a requirement. He requires that we accept our salvation on faith, as a gift not based on works but by grace. In doing so, we demonstrate our confidence that God is true to his word and will forgive our sins. In doing so, we demonstrate our trust that God does not favor certain individuals over others. In doing so, we receive from him the complete remission of our sins and are made righteous in his sight.

Additional Reading

Read from *Faith - The Link With God's Power*
chapter 2 on pages 57-63
chapter 6 on pages 64-70
chapter 13 on pages 87-93
chapter 14 on pages 94-101
of the book passage compilation

Module I
Lesson 5:
Salvation as a Doctrine and Experience
(continued)

References: *Time Is Running Out* and *Faith - The Link With God's Power*

I.5.1. Salvation's Nature

We cannot save ourselves. Faith in Jesus Christ is a saving grace through which we receive, and rest upon, the remission of our sins. A sinner, out of recognition of his own guilt and in apprehension of the judgment which he deserves, can reach out to a loving and forgiving Creator only because the debt of the sin was paid through the atoning sacrifice of God's son. (John 1:12, Acts 16:31, Ephesians 1:7)

The concept of salvation is unclear to many people because they have no idea what they are being saved from nor do they grasp the reality that they need to be saved. "It is futile to preach that Jesus saves if people are not in danger - or if they do not know they are in danger." (*Time Is Running Out*)

When Adam and Eve sinned, humanity was separated from its relationship with the Creator. Though the immediate consequence of their sin was expulsion from the Garden of Eden, the real punishment was the loss of intimacy with God. A sinful mankind could no longer experience the enjoyment of the presence of a sinless God. (Isaiah 59:2) There was nothing mankind could do to make amends for the sin and, since that time, all efforts to make recompense for sin have been fruitless and inadequate. Only the one who has been wronged can truly provide forgiveness.

Nevertheless, God loves his creation (Jeremiah 31:3) and longs to have a personal relationship with everyone, regardless of their sin. But a perfect God cannot have intimacy with an imperfect humanity. (Habakkuk 1:13) Though man may endeavor to cover or change his sinful nature, he still remains imperfect and his efforts do not equate with the perfection and holiness of God. Therefore, Jesus Christ, perfect in every way, took upon himself the imperfections and sins of the world in order for man to be made righteous in God's sight. (2 Corinthians 5:21) Without Christ's death and resurrection, man's future is eternal damnation in hell. Through Christ's death and resurrection, man has the assurance of eternal life. (Ephesians 1:7)

I.5.1.1.   Eternal Destiny Changed

Salvation is the key to change mankind's eternal destiny. It is not a cure-all or resolution for everything that happens in an individual's life. Rather, it provides the means whereby the individual can be freed from the burden and guilt of sin and made pure in God's sight. The plan of salvation which God established through his son now guarantees eternal life and gives mankind confidence in his own eternal reward. That changed eternal destiny is not dependant upon the individual's works, nor does it require that the individual be good enough to merit God's favor. Simply, it makes amends for the individual's sin and brings about the forgiveness of God and the justification of mankind. (Romans 3:24, Romans 5:18, Romans 6:23)

I.5.1.2.   The Changed Heart

When an individual comes face-to-face with his own sinful nature and has repented of the sins in his heart, he is made a new creature in God's sight. (2 Corinthians 5:17) In sin, the heart produces sin (Matthew 15:19). In salvation, the heart is made pure and the desires of man are focused on serving and pleasing God. No longer is the progression of mankind toward self-indulgence and gratification, but, rather, the goal is relationship with God that is pleasing and righteous. (Romans 10:10)

I.5.1.3.   The Changed Life

The forgiving grace of God brings a change in the lives of those who are saved. No longer bound by the chains of the sinful nature, mankind is free to fulfill the call God has placed on his life. The individual's personal wants and lifestyles become secondary to the primary desire to follow Christ. The lust of the flesh, the lust of the eyes, and the pride of life are no longer part of the believer's lifestyle. (1 John 2:16) Sin cannot abide in a vessel that is committed to God. Rather, the forgiven life produces fruit which reflects the very nature of God. (Galatians 5:22-23)

I.5.1.4.   Confidence in Life – Hope in Death

Released from the bondage of sin, the redeemed are now able to walk in the joy and assurance of their freedom through Christ. Theirs is a life filled with the confidence of God's love and the promise of grace in death. No longer condemned for his sins, the believer can now bask in the joy of victory over death. (Romans 8:1)

I.5.2.   The Life of the Believer

The believer's life is more than just "saved by grace." Though "works" cannot bring about salvation, the "works" of the believer following salvation should be evidence of, or testimony to, the change that has occurred in the believer's life. The believer has a responsibility to live a life that is pleasing to God and that bears fruit in bringing other lost souls into the Kingdom of Heaven. Jesus told his disciples that those to whom much is given (salvation), much is required (service and ministry) (Luke 12:48).

I.5.2.1.   Holiness

"I beseech you therefore brethren, by the mercies of God, that ye present your bodies a living sacrifice, holy, acceptable unto God, which is your reasonable service. And be not conformed to this world: but be ye transformed by the renewing of your mind, that ye may prove what is that good, and acceptable, and perfect, will of God." (Romans 12:1-2)

The believer is called to a life of holiness, transformed by the grace and power of the Holy Spirit. Holiness is not a requirement to receive salvation, but it is a requirement of salvation. It is, and should be, a natural result of the remission of sins. Holiness is not just being pious or religious. It encompasses a change in lifestyle. The believer's life should mirror the image of Christ, following the example that he set by putting others before himself. Holiness is a life of sacrifice and giving. It is a life of forbearance, accepting and enduring the actions of others, whether in deliberate acts of rebellion and persecution or through unintentional acts of ignorance. It is a life committed to righteousness and service, forsaking all else.

Additional Reading

Read from *Time Is Running Out*
passages from chapter 13 on pages 33-39
of the book passage compilation

I.5.2.2.   Worship

David wrote in Psalm 29:2 *"Give unto the Lord the glory due unto his name; worship the Lord in the beauty of holiness."* An integral part of the believer's life is the time he commits to worshipping the Lord. The Psalms are full of songs of praise, thanksgiving and adoration. The Lord desires and deserves it; the believer needs it.

When considering the magnitude of the agony of Calvary, a remorseful creation should fall to its knees in gratitude. There is no sufficient explanation for the sacrifice of Christ other than the love of God for his creation. *"Behold, what manner of love the Father hath bestowed upon us, that we should be called the sons of God."* (1 John 3:1a)

I.5.2.3. Ministry

"When considering the scope and ramifications of the Great Commission, one cannot help but be indelibly impressed by the fact that it is an expression of the love of God to the whole world. That is why, whatever his or her career, the Christian's main business is evangelism." (*Time Is Running Out*)

Evangelist Bonnke strongly believes that every Christian, in accepting salvation, must also accept the responsibility to evangelize. That is not to say that every believer is called of God to go to a distant land to preach the gospel of Jesus Christ. Rather, every believer is called of God to preach the gospel of Jesus Christ to everyone with whom that believer has contact.

But God does not throw his children into an evangelistic maelstrom without any help. Through the Holy Spirit he empowers us to withstand the attacks of Satan and to speak with boldness and authority. Ours is not a gospel of weakness and frail timidity. Ours is a gospel of power and strength. Jesus told his disciples, *"tarry ... until ye be endued with power from on high"* (Luke 24:49) and *"ye shall receive power, after that the Holy Ghost is come upon you: and ye shall be witnesses unto me both in Jerusalem, and in all Judea, and in Samaria, and unto the uttermost part of the earth."* (Acts 1:8)

Power. You will receive power. You will be witnesses. That doesn't sound like a weak, apologetic milquetoast, afraid of others, afraid of what they may think, say or do. You will receive power and be witnesses. There is no "if" in that statement. There is no "maybe." There is no other option. You **will** receive power - that's a statement of fact. You **will** be witnesses – that's a statement of command. Jesus is not asking for a vote to decide whether or not we want to do this. As believers, it is not our option ... it is our mandate ... it is our destiny.

Evangelist Bonnke has likened faith to a wiring system that carries power into our lives. The wiring carries the power, but it does not create it. "Faith in itself is not power, but it links us to the power source." (*Faith – the Link with God's Power*) Power is given to the believer for action – to give the believer the resources to be able to minister to others. Consider 1 Timothy 1:7: *"For God hath not given us the spirit of fear; but of power and of love, and of a sound mind."* With that power, the believer is enabled to effectively fulfill the call to action to evangelize the world.

Additional Reading

Read from *Faith – The Link With God's Power*
chapter 27 on pages 117-125 of the book passage compilation

Module II
Lesson 6:
The Biblical Foundation for Evangelism

References: *Evangelism By Fire* and *Faith - The Link With God's Power*

"The command to evangelize is all that matters, snatching men from the flames of hell. That divine command was not given in a passing mood of the Lord. God Himself is driven by the peril in which human beings stand without Christ. Calvary was His imperative!" (*Evangelism By Fire*) Consider John 10:16: *"And other sheep I have which are not of this fold; them also I must bring, and they will hear My voice: and there will be one flock and one shepherd."* It is not the desire nor will of God that any of his creation be lost. His command to mankind is to *"go ye into all the world and preach the gospel to every creature"* (Mark 16:15).

II.6.1.   The Attributes of God

II.6.1.1.   God is Omnipotent

God has unlimited or universal power and authority. He is not bound by the limitations with which mankind must contend. Rather, his power, his authority, transcends all others. He is the Almighty God, the *El Shaddai* (Genesis 17:1). He does not contend with physical, mental, or emotional limitations. Job confessed, *"I know that thou canst do every thing"* (Job 42:2). Jesus declared, *"with God all things are possible"* (Matthew 19:26b). Nature itself quakes at the voice of God and is submissive to his will, as evidenced by Christ calming the sea (Matthew 8, Mark 4, Luke 8).

II.6.1.2.   God is Omniscient

God knows all things. He knows himself thoroughly and completely
and knows all that exists beyond his being. There is nothing of
mankind that can be hidden from God or is unknown to him. He is
aware of every creature, every need, every struggle. Scripture declares
that he even knows the number of hairs on our heads (Luke 12:7).
Mankind should tremble at the realization that an omniscient God
knows our every thoughts and deeds, even those which we attempt
to keep secret or hidden. His knowledge is unlimited; his wisdom is
perfect.

II.6.1.3.   God is Omnipresent

God is present everywhere. He is with the laborer in the fields, the
mother in childbirth and the family mourning the loss of a loved
one, all at the same time. There is no one who is beyond the presence
of God. Consider Jeremiah 23:23-24: *"Am I a God at hand, saith the
Lord, and not a God afar off? Can any hide himself in secret places that
I shall not see him? saith the Lord."* This concept is difficult to grasp by
the limitations of human rationality and reasoning. It is the kind of
stuff that science fiction authors write about. Nevertheless, it is not
fiction, scientific or otherwise. God is with you even as you read this
text, just as he is with everyone else at this same moment. He knows
every thought you have and he is with you wherever you go. How that
should impact the actions of mankind! There is no secret hidden from
God.

II.6.1.4.   God is Immutable

God never changes. He is now, always has been and ever will be
Jehovah Elohim (the Lord God). He does not change his will on a
whim. He never changes toward his own. He never varies. His love is
perfect. His works show that he is *"the same yesterday, and today, and
forever"* (Hebrews 13:8).

II.6.2.   The Nature of God

The nature of God is best explained by the simple, yet eloquent, proclamation of John 3:16: *"For God so loved the world, that he gave his only begotten Son, that whosoever believeth in him should not perish, but have everlasting life."* Scripture is replete with passages that focus on God's love for his creation, specifically, his compassion for the lost. "The character of God is one of concern, goodwill, and action. Jesus performs ten thousand wonders every hour of every day ... His character outshines all that is ever pictured in men, women, or myth" (*Faith - The Link With God's Power*).

In his love for mankind, God has declared that we are his children, the sons of God (1 John 3:1-2). As any good parent sacrificially provides for the well-being of his children, so God also gives his best that his children should not suffer and perish. God's ultimate sacrifice for his children was the crucifixion of Jesus Christ, God's son, so that humanity could be saved from the eternal destruction of hell. God will not be mocked. With the gift of life that he gives, he also requires that those who receive live a life pleasing to him and in accordance with his word.

It is not within the power of mankind to save itself. Man has tried. Nevertheless, all efforts to be like God or to strive to attain god-like powers have resulted in destruction and failure (Tower of Babel, Genesis 11; Simon the Sorcerer, Acts 8).

The *Westminster Shorter Catechism* describes God as "spirit, infinite, eternal, and unchangeable, in his being, power, holiness, justice, goodness, and truth". Consider some of the aspects of God's nature.

God is Spirit

"God is a Spirit: and they that worship him must worship him in spirit and in truth." (John 4:24)

God is Eternal

"Now unto the King eternal, immortal, invisible, the only wise God, be honour and glory for ever and ever. Amen." (1 Timothy 1:17)

God is Light

"This then is the message which we have heard of him, and declare unto you, that God is light, and in him is no darkness at all." (1 John 1:5)

God is Love

"He that loveth not knoweth not God; for God is love." (1 John 4:8)

Additional Reading

**Reread from *Faith – The Link With God's Power*
chapter 13 on pages 87-93 of the book passage compilation**

Module II
Lesson 7:
The Biblical Foundation for Evangelism
(continued)

Reference: *Faith - The Link With God's Power*

II.7.1.   The Old Testament Provision for Sojourners

God loves his creation. His desire is for all to be saved. He has anointed the church with power to preach the gospel to every nation. This is not a new revelation. In the Old Testament, there are numerous examples of God's desire to save from destruction. He called Israel to be the vehicle through which salvation would come. Abraham was called, not just to be the father of a great nation, but to be an instrument of blessing to the world (Genesis 12). Israel was unique in its calling, but it was destined for a purpose far greater than what it understood as its destiny.

God's compassion is evident throughout the Old Testament. When considering the destruction of Sodom, God was willing to listen to Abraham's plea for mercy if only ten righteous could be found (Genesis 18). Regretfully, even ten was too high and the city perished. But, it did not perish until after Lot and his family had been rescued (Genesis 19). Though Abraham pleaded for Sodom, God's judgment came, but Lot was saved.

Throughout Old Testament history, the way of salvation was provided through the sacrificial lamb. That lamb, innocent of sin, had to die in order to make recompense for the sins of mankind. That lamb, however, was insufficient for a lasting forgiveness and a new sacrifice had to be offered each year. God, in the compassion of his nature and love, promised a deliverer who would take upon himself the sins of the world and provide, once and for all, eternal forgiveness for sin.

The prophets of the Old Testament foretold of the coming of this messiah, describing his suffering and giving Israel a hope of a better future and a restoration of full relationship with God. This promised redeemer would not only forgive the sins of the world, he would usher Israel into a new era or destiny. Isaiah spoke of a rod out of the stem of Jesse (Isaiah 11:1). Jeremiah proclaimed the coming of a righteous branch (Jeremiah 23:5). Micah foretold the coming of a ruler in Israel (Micah 5:2). Though Israel gloried in self-righteousness at the thoughts of a coming king, the people seemed to overlook the reality of the suffering the king would have to endure (Isaiah 53).

God's judgment is inevitable. Consider Psalm 9:7: *"But the Lord shall endure for ever: he hath prepared his throne for judgment."* Too often, the world fails to grasp the magnitude of the judgment of God. In his perfect time, God will bring everything into final judgment (Ecclesiastes 12:14). Until God's final judgment comes, he still expects his followers to do all they can to lead others into a saving knowledge of faith in the Lord Jesus Christ.

Additional Reading

Read from *Faith – The Link With God's Power*
chapter 11 on pages 71-78
chapter 12 on pages 79-86
of the book passage compilation

Module II
Lesson 8:
The Biblical Foundation for Evangelism
(continued)

Reference: *Evangelism By Fire*

II.8.1.   The New Testament

"For unto you is born this day in the city of David a Saviour,
which is Christ the Lord."
Luke 2:11

The promised redeemer of Isaiah was fulfilled through the birth
of Jesus Christ. The angels of heaven announced his birth and
proclaimed his deity. Shepherds and kings paid homage to him,
bowing in adoration and wonder at the feet of the child who had been
sent to take upon himself the sins of the world. It was inconceivable
that this small child in Bethlehem would one day accept in his flesh
the pain and agony of sin, yielding his life as the propitiation for the
rebellion of mankind. It was beyond the realm of consideration that
the innocent babe, full of promise, had to die so that those who are
guilty might live.

The ministry of Jesus Christ completed God's plan of redemption.
The agony of Gethsemane and the horror of Calvary were defeated by
the power and beauty of the resurrection. Jesus promised the coming
of the Holy Spirit and proclaimed to his followers that they now had
a new commission, a great commission, to proclaim the gospel to
all the world (Acts 1:8). The promised Messiah had come; now, the
responsibility to draw the world to that Messiah was laid upon those
who believed. Theirs would not be an easy task; nevertheless, it was a
task they could not forsake.

The "power" came at Pentecost and the followers of Christ were empowered with new strength and a new boldness to preach the eternal gospel of salvation through Jesus Christ. Peter, who had denied knowing Jesus for fear of his own safety, boldly stood in the midst of the people, no longer bound by fear, and declared that Jesus was the Christ (Acts 2). The gospel had to be proclaimed. Those who were witness to it could not sit idly by and wait for someone else to speak. They had a message for the world. The redemption of mankind was now their responsibility.

The first century church committed itself to spreading the gospel to the known world. It was not easy. Paul, and so many like him, suffered through hardships, attacks, imprisonments, and death – all in the name of Christ and all in an attempt to tell mankind that Jesus Christ had brought redemption to a lost and dying world. But it was more than just preaching the gospel. It was a reproduction of life. Each new convert was nurtured, mentored and commissioned to go forth. The calling given to each follower was not to sit; rather, it was to go, to do, to work, to harvest. Salvation was not theirs to enjoy alone. With the blessing and assurance of salvation comes the responsibility of evangelism.

Additional Reading

**Read from *Evangelism By Fire*
chapter 5 on pages 129-138 of the book passage compilation**

II.8.2.   Power for Evangelism

When Jesus ascended into heaven, leaving his disciples, he knew their weaknesses. He had seen them all in action in the three years of his ministry on earth; he knew their personalities. He had seen Peter sleep during Jesus' personal agony in Gethsemane, awaken with an intensity for battle that resulted in injury to Malchus, the servant of the high priest, and, then, deny any knowledge of the Christ (John 18). Jesus knew his disciples. He knew they needed anointing and power to enable them to now fulfill their purpose in ministry, to spread the gospel news of Jesus Christ. So, he told them to *"wait for the promise of the Father ... but ye shall be baptized with the Holy Ghost"* (Acts 1:4-5).

The disciples were often impulsive and even, at times, irrational. Surely, "waiting" for something they couldn't comprehend was agony. What did it mean when Christ said, "ye shall be baptized with the Holy Ghost"? Water baptism they understood. Baptism with the Holy Ghost? That was most assuredly a phrase they didn't understand. How would they know when they had been baptized? Earlier he had told Peter, "Feed my sheep" (John 21:17). But now, Jesus said, "wait" and wait they must.

"But ye shall receive power, after that the Holy Ghost is come upon you" (Acts 1:8). Power. What kind of power? What did that power mean? All they knew was Jesus had told them to wait, that they would receive power, and they would be witnesses.

Then, on the day of Pentecost, the promise of the risen and ascended Lord was fulfilled. Not what the disciples were looking for, perhaps, but, most definitely, what they needed. With the outpouring of the Holy Ghost (Acts 2), there was a new strength, a new desire, and a new purpose. Through the outpouring, the disciples were changed. No longer were they weak and fearful; they were emboldened for ministry. They were changed; the world, through them, has never been the same.

As you read the book of Acts, each event, each journey, demonstrates anew how that power received at Pentecost made evangelists out of simple fishermen. Men who previously had no voice were boldly proclaiming the message of salvation through Jesus Christ with intensity, authority and, most notably, power.

The power received at Pentecost was not just for the disciples alone. Though they were the initial recipients of the power, it was actually given to enable them to fulfill the great commission that Christ had proclaimed as their ministry, mission and destiny. It was not theirs to keep. Rather, it was theirs to use in declaring the death and resurrection of the Messiah and what that meant for all mankind.

The blessings of Pentecost ushered in a new era; this was the beginning of God's plan of evangelism. The disciples were told to wait and that they would receive power. Power for what? Power to be *"witnesses unto me both in Jerusalem, and in all Judea, and in Samaria, and unto the uttermost part of the earth"* (Acts 1:8). Jesus very clearly delineated that the gospel message was not just an immediate blessing for the disciples only. He gave clear instructions as to where the message should be shared. And, lest there be any doubt or confusion, he declared that the gospel was for all.

II.8.2.1.   Jerusalem

The disciples were told to tarry (to wait) in Jerusalem. Then, after they had received power, their first field of evangelism was to be their own community or environment. Believers are to be witnesses in their own homes, families and towns.

II.8.2.2.   Judea

Jerusalem was located in Judea. Judea represented the Hebrew or Jewish culture and people. The witness of the disciples was to be more than just a local endeavor. It had a national perspective.

II.8.2.3.   Samaria

To the devout Jew, Samaritans were traitors who had rejected their Hebrew faith and had inter-married with Gentiles. Devout Jews disdained having anything to do with Gentiles, but, from their perspective, Samaritans were even worse than Gentiles. Gentiles were not of the chosen people; Samaritans had betrayed the faith ... and that was far worse. Nevertheless, the gospel message was to go beyond national boundaries and even reach to the unloved, the rejected, the repulsed.

II.8.2.4.   Uttermost Part of the Earth

Lest there be any doubt of the mission of the disciples, Jesus, in essence, summarized the mission with this one simple phrase. The power was not the possession of the disciples. It was to be used by them to take the gospel message throughout the entire world. Jew, Samaritan, Gentile ... it didn't matter. All were to be told, to be evangelized, and power was given to make it possible to do so.

On that very day, Peter began the work by preaching to the people who had gathered in Jerusalem (Acts 2:14-40). *"... and the same day there were added unto them about three thousand souls"* (Acts 2:41). How exciting to consider that the first sermon preached after Holy Spirit power had been received resulted in the saving of three thousand people. The fire (power) was given at Pentecost and this first harvest of souls fanned the very flames of evangelism, showing the disciples the impact of what they had received. Power had been given, lives were being changed, and the call to evangelize had started. The purpose of the Great Commission was a reality.

Additional Reading

**Read from *Evangelism By Fire*
chapter 6 on pages 139-144 of the book passage compilation**

Module II
Lesson 9:
The biblical Foundation for Evangelism
(continued)

References: *Evangelism By Fire* and *Faith – The Link With God's Power*

II.9.1.   Models for personal and public Evangelism

Twenty-first century evangelists have the benefit of reviewing and learning from the acts of earlier evangelists. First century evangelists walked paths that had never been traveled before. They could not look to someone else as an example. Religions abounded throughout the world but no other religion sought to spread its message to the entire world with such zeal, energy, and determination. When one nation conquered another, the vanquished were usually forced to submit to the religious perspective of the victor. Religious views changed depending on the whims of the strongest military. Often, religions transitioned as tenets from one were incorporated into the beliefs of another.

Christianity was different. It did not seek to overthrow nations. It did not seek to blend with other beliefs. It came with a servant message and stood firm in the face of adversity and persecution. To many, it probably seemed to be weak, but the resolution of its adherents to spread the gospel withstood any assault the world could offer. The gospel message of Christ was new, different, and impacted the world as no other religion had been able to do, proving its power and truth.

II.9.1.1.   Philip in Samaria

The first recorded evangelist in the New Testament was Philip. He
was one of the *"seven men of honest report, full of the Holy Ghost and
wisdom"* (Acts 6:1-6) who was set apart by the disciples, appointed
to oversee taking care of the widows and children in the church at
Jerusalem. However, after the martyrdom of Stephen (Acts 7) and the
intensifying of the persecution of the church, Philip became more
active in evangelistic ministry, preaching the gospel in Samaria
(Acts 8).

Philip's ministry in Samaria was extremely effective. He cast out
devils and healed the lame and palsied, just as the apostles had
done. *"And the people with one accord gave heed unto those things which
Philip spake ..."* (Acts 8:6). His is the first account of ministry beyond
Jerusalem and Judea ... into Samaria. Remember the commission of
Christ to be *"witnesses unto me* [Christ] *both in Jerusalem, and in all
Judea, and in Samaria, and unto the uttermost part of the earth"*? The
commission was being fulfilled. The witness in Samaria was just the
beginning. Other evangelist forays were still to come.

One who was notably impacted by Philip's ministry in Samaria was
Simon the magician. *"Then Simon himself believed also: and when he
was baptized, he continued with Philip, and wondered, beholding the
miracles and signs which were done"* (Acts 8:13). However, when Simon
saw people receiving the Holy Ghost after the apostles had laid hands
on them, Simon sought to purchase this power and received a strong
rebuke from Peter (Acts 8:14-24).

Additional Reading

**Reread from *Faith – The Link With God's Power*
chapter 27 on pages 117-125 of the book passage compilation**

II.9.1.2.   Philip in Gaza

Philip was told by an angel to go to Gaza where the Holy Spirit directed him to an encounter with an Ethiopian eunuch (Acts 8:26-39). This shows the diversity of evangelism from preaching to the masses (as had been done in Samaria) to one-on-one personal evangelistic outreach. With power, Philip was able to explain to the Ethiopian eunuch the meanings of the writings of Isaiah and the fulfillment of Isaiah's prophecies through Jesus Christ. The Scriptures tell us that Philip *"preached unto him Jesus"* (Acts 8:35b). Through Philip's witnessing to the Ethiopian eunuch, the man believed in Jesus Christ as the Son of God and was baptized. As soon as the man was baptized, the Holy Spirit *"caught away Philip, that the eunuch saw him no more"* (Acts 8:39). What an incredible example of God's power! Philip was there and then he was gone. The eunuch went away rejoicing and Philip continued to preach wherever he was directed (Acts 8:39b-40).

We do not know the impact the Ethiopian eunuch may have had on others. Certainly, however, it is noteworthy that he was from beyond the boundaries of Jerusalem, Judea and Samaria. The evangelism of the gospel was gaining strength and expanding.

II.9.1.3.   Paul

The book of Acts is filled with accounts of how the followers of Christ fulfilled the call to "go" and "preach" the gospel. Consider Paul's missionary experiences in Philippi (in Macedonia, well beyond Jerusalem, Judea, and Samaria). He preached and Lydia, a seller of purple cloth, was converted (Acts 16:14-15). A girl possessed with an evil spirit tried to hinder his evangelism and, through the power of the Holy Spirit, Paul cast out the demon that bound her (Acts 16:16-18). This did not please her masters and, subsequently, Paul and Silas were arrested and thrown in prison. While in prison, and through a series of miraculous events, Paul and Silas were able to witness to the jailer (and ultimately his entire family) and they all were saved (Acts 16:19-34). Paul used every experience as an opportunity to witness for Christ and to lead others to salvation. The Satanic attempts to stop the spread of the gospel were thwarted.

Before his conversion, Paul had been filled with fury against the believers. Now, empowered by the Holy Spirit, he was undaunted in his intent to tell the world the good news of Jesus Christ. The beatings, the threats, the imprisonment ... none of these could stop Paul in his mission. Prison was just another venue in which to witness the saving miracles of God. Surely, the jailer did not expect to be confronted with his creator that night. And what of the other prisoners? One can only imagine the impact on their lives when God's power was manifest.

Did Paul fear during his evangelistic travels? Most assuredly, he did. In his first letter to the church at Corinth, he speaks of his fear. *"I was with you in weakness, and in fear, and in much trembling"* (1 Corinthians 2:3). Yet, through the power of the Holy Spirit, he was given boldness that enabled him to overcome his fears, no matter what circumstances he was facing, and he was able to preach with authority and conviction, for Paul knew that God was with him.

Additional Reading

Read from *Evangelism by Fire*
chapter 14 on pages 153-162 of the book passage compilation

Module II
Lesson 10:
The Biblical Foundation for Evangelism
(continued)

Reference: *Evangelism By Fire*

II.10.1.   The Church and Evangelism

"As long as the Church emphasizes the Baptism in the Spirit, the
Holy Spirit will stimulate evangelism and missions. It is the same as
a flower: Holy Spirit-evangelism carries in itself the seeds of its own
perpetuity and increase." (*Evangelism By Fire*)

Those who have chosen to follow Christ are drawn into a new
fellowship and a new relationship with one another. They have
become a new people with a new identity, the church. They used
the Greek term, *ecclesia* (assembly or congregation), to identify
themselves. As the community of believers has increased, the purpose
of the church has taken on a much more global perspective in its
ministry endeavors. Though denominational perspectives have, at
times, caused division, the purpose of the church united still stands.
The church remains a foundational support and accountability for
those who "go" and provides discipleship and training for those who
are new in their faith. No one can say that he has finished the work.
World evangelism is a team effort and every member of the team is
critical for the success of the mission.

"World outreach today needs, and always has needed, those who are
willing to go down and those who are willing to hold the rope! That
rope is a lifeline." (*Evangelism By Fire*)

Additional Reading

Read from *Evangelism By Fire*
chapter 7 on pages 145-152
chapter 18 on pages 172-177
of the book passage compilation

Module III
Lesson 11:
Principles of Global Evangelism

Reference: *Evangelism By Fire*

The first two modules focused on the theology and nature of salvation and evangelism. Those modules provided the foundation and justification for the importance of evangelism. With that foundation established, we now turn our attention to the practices and principles of global evangelism. This module will focus on the specifics of both crusade evangelism and evangelism for church growth.

In 2 Timothy 4, the apostle Paul wrote strong words of encouragement to Timothy, not knowing if they would see each other again. Paul exhorted the young preacher to "do the work of an evangelist" (2 Timothy 4:5). The inclusion of evangelism in Paul's charge to Timothy emphasizes its importance. Other aspects of ministry had been addressed in Paul's previous correspondence. But now, as he is giving his final charge, he leaves no doubt as to the significance of the evangelistic ministry.

III.11.1. Preaching Crusades

One of the foremost international evangelists today is Reinhard Bonnke. His crusades have drawn millions of people to a saving knowledge of Jesus Christ. But not every evangelist will have crusades like Reinhard Bonnke. That, however, should not diminish the zeal and efforts of ministries to have evangelistic crusades.

Quite possibly, one of the biggest stumbling blocks to successful preaching crusades is lack of sufficient preparation and organization. Regardless of the size of the crusade, adequate preparation is essential. Lack of preparation does not prohibit God's ability to move; it can, however, limit the evangelist's effectiveness to truly move in the anointing of the Holy Spirit and indicates a cavalier attitude toward the gospel message.

III.11.1.1. Preparing the Evangelist

As the leader of the crusade, the evangelist has a pivotal role in the success of the ministry. It is through his leadership, charisma and ministry style that the crusade gains much of its impact and drive. It is the evangelist who must carry the burden to inspire and motivate his workers. Those who are helping with the crusade will only be as enthused as that demonstrated by their leader.

With such a powerful and responsible burden of leadership on the shoulders of one individual, that individual must be cautious, lest he become side-tracked in his focus, or develop a wrong perspective of his role in the ministry. The evangelist must be an individual of integrity – at all levels. There are three great dangers that can impact an evangelist's effectiveness: money, sex, and ego. Let's consider each of these.

III.11.1.1.1. Money

Every crusade involves and requires some type of financial accountability. Inevitably, there will be fees and permits to pay, venue rental, utilities, salaries, travel expenses, publicity costs, equipment, lodging, food, and follow-up expenses. To mount a crusade of any size is costly, requiring a substantial amount of money to cover the expenditures. The offerings (and other financial resources, i.e., gifts, book/tape sales, etc.) must cover those expenses. This is sound fiscal responsibility. As a ministry grows, its financial needs increase, often in proportion with the gifts and offerings it receives.

The evangelist's income must be commensurate with the amount of funding coming into the ministry. There's nothing wrong with that. *"The labourer is worthy of his hire"* (Luke 10:7). The caution, however, is that the increase in financial resources can be instrumental in causing some individuals to make the "income" a higher goal than the salvation of souls.

Paul wrote Timothy, *"For the love of money is the root of all evil ..."* (1 Timothy 6:10). That is not to say that money is the sin; rather, it's the priority that is given to money, and attaining money, that causes men to sin. For the evangelist, the financial gains can lead to a style of living that requires more resources and it becomes more and more difficult to sacrifice lifestyle when the resources are not available.

Also, there may be times when ungodly (or spiritually immature) individuals may try to use money to gain favor, prestige or power. In essence, the evangelist must be wary of individuals who provide financial resources for the ministry with inappropriate expectations attached to the gift. It's critical that the evangelist guard himself against the lures of monetary gain, lest his ministry be compromised.

Additional Reading

Read from *Evangelism By Fire*
chapter 17 on pages 163-171 of the book passage compilation

Module III
Lesson 12
Principles of Global Evangelism (continued)

References: *Evangelism By Fire* and *Faith - The Link With God's Power*

III.12.1.   Preaching Crusades (continued)

III.12.1.1.   Preparing the Evangelist (continued)

III.12.1.1.2. Sex

Regretfully, there are individuals who, for any number of reasons, may identify the evangelist as a god-like figure, someone to be almost idolized. This is not necessarily their intent, but as the evangelist's ministry is effective, people are drawn to the evangelist and equate the evangelist with the power he is able to manifest. As they are blessed, their desire is to be close to the evangelist, to glean from the evangelist's ministry, and to serve the evangelist, repaying the evangelist for the blessings received. In their desire to give back to the evangelist, they are often willing to do anything, including providing sexual favors. Sometimes, the follower will project onto the evangelist a psychological need for acceptance and in seeking that acceptance no sacrifice of self is unreasonable and inappropriate.

This is troublesome in several ways. An evangelist that is not solid, grounded in his spiritual walk, may easily fall prey to the lusts that accompany such offerings or may actually prey on the weaknesses of those striving for his attention and affection. On the other hand, the follower may feel the way to truly provide for the evangelist, either due to gratitude, idolatry, or confusion, is to give in to sexual desires or actions. In this way, the follower is demonstrating his or her complete trust in the evangelist.

There are many accounts of ministries that have been toppled due to the sexual liaisons of the evangelist and/or those in ministry leadership. For the evangelist who is tired and lonely from being on the road and away from home, the sexual favors offered by a willing and attractive follower are often wrongfully justified as "meeting the evangelist's needs."

Satan knows the physical desires and weaknesses of mankind. He will use whatever means he can to destroy an evangelist's ministry. Since sexual sins are most often committed in private, Satan will delude the participants into thinking they are hurting no one and there is no harm in what they are doing. The Bible is clear on this, however. Fornication (i.e., sexual acts between individuals who are not married) is sin. There is no middle road. There are no examples of times when this might be allowed. As the spiritual leader, the evangelist must live a life above reproach and though temptations may come, he cannot yield to those temptations, nor can he allow such dalliances to be a part of his ministry.

III.12.1.1.3. Ego

An individual's pride can be a very destructive thing. The evangelist must be especially wary of the potential for prideful attitudes. There's a difference between pride and self-confidence. As you go forth in evangelistic ministry, you can be confident in the promises of God and know that he will supply your needs. That's not pride ... that's faith. Nevertheless, the evangelist must be cautious lest he put more faith in his own efforts and less in the power of God. As a ministry grows, there is the inclination, if one is not careful, to begin to look at "what I have done" rather than "what God has done." That exaltation of one's self-image, ego, can birth a pride that is sinful and destructive.

In the evangelistic crusades, the evangelist is the primary vehicle for bringing God's blessings to the people. After all the planning, the music and the worship, the evangelist brings the Word of God and it is the impact of that Word that brings to fruition the harvest of souls. Undeniably, there will be people who are saved through the effects of the other aspects of the ministry. The largest response, however, will be from the spoken Word of God. When there are people who are coming just to hear the evangelist preach, there is the potential for self-pride to grow. That's what Satan wants. He wants to play on the evangelist's ego. After all, that was Satan's downfall. His pride and desire to exalt himself led to his expulsion from heaven (Isaiah 14:12-15). He knows the destructiveness of pride and will use that to attempt to destroy an evangelist's effectiveness in ministry.

But, Satan is crafty. He does not approach the evangelist with pride from the start. Rather, he will appreciate the ministry success the evangelist may have. He will delight in the financial resources that may come. He will relish the fame and prominence that may result in successful crusades. Then, using all of those he will feed into the evangelist's ego, planting the seeds of pride, knowing that pride will ultimately bring down the evangelist and destroy the ministry. He will use money. He will use sexual relationships. He will do all he can to build the ego of the evangelist, telling him, in his own mind that he, the evangelist, is the source of the success and deserves the accolades and favor. Sometimes the evangelist may not fall prey to the temptations of money and sex; he might, however, become victim to self-pride and its impact.

All of the dangers an evangelist might face should not be seen as reasons for avoiding the call to evangelize. The potential for each of these can be evident in anyone's life, not just the evangelist. How does the evangelist prepare himself to fight against these dangers? Quite simply, he prays, studies the Bible, and puts on the armor of God – daily. Sounds simple? It really is. There is not a magic formula. The evangelist (and anyone for that matter) can resist the Satanic temptations by keeping his focus on God first and letting everything else be secondary.

Additional Reading

Read from *Evangelism By Fire*
chapter 19 on pages 178-186
Faith – The Link With God's Power
chapter 23 on pages 109-116
of the book passage compilation

Module III
Lesson 13
Principles of Global Evangelism (continued)

Reference: *Evangelism By Fire*

III.13.1. Preaching Crusades (continued)

III.13.1.1. Preparing the Soil

The evangelist must be personally prepared for the crusade. As he is getting prepared, he must lead others in working with local churches and leaders to prepare the spiritual hearts of the people to receive the Word of God and to take care of the myriad of details that must be faced. Even before the actual logistics of the crusade are considered, it is critical that the local believers be brought together to provide the prayer support necessary for the success of the meeting. A team must be gathered and workers must be trained.

III.13.1.1.1. Local Churches / Leader

Recruit local churches, pastors and laymen to take a leadership role in the crusade. This has a two-fold purpose. One, their connections with the community will make it easier to get the word out that the crusade is being held. Some of these leaders may also have contacts with local authorities who have to grant permits and licenses for the event. Second, this provides a large pool of local people who can take on the burden of the preliminary planning and the follow-up. These are important people and their influence and role should neither be overlooked nor minimized. The support of the local church leaders can make the logistics much easier to handle and can provide a large resource of people to perform the many tasks that need to be done.

As you gain the support and involvement of the local church leadership, include them in the planning process. Do not just tell them what you need them to do. Listen to their input. They know the community. They know the need. They know the mores and values of the people to whom you will be ministering. Do not treat them as servants or hired workers; rather, enlist them as co-laborers in the crusade. Their support is critical to the success of the crusade and their lack of support (most often coming from failure to include them in the planning and execution of the crusade) can also be instrumental in inhibiting the crusade's success. The local church is a wonderful resource and should not be overlooked. They are the true laborers in the field and failing to include them is tantamount to insulting them and the work they do.

Support the leadership in their endeavors. Give credit to the pastors and leaders for the work they have been doing. Find out what you can do to help them ... not just what they need to do to help your crusade. Even before the crusade starts make plans to give recognition to the churches and leaders who have assisted and to encourage the converts to go to the local churches for support, teaching, and discipleship. As the local churches take on the various planning roles, get updates from them, praise their accomplishments and offer suggestions in areas where they may be struggling.

Above all, affirm them and pray for them. This isn't saying that you have to treat the leaders as children who don't know what to do. Quite the contrary! They are the experts on the community and should be recognized as such. Encourage them. Learn their strengths and weaknesses and give them tasks that are within the sphere of capabilities. Set them up for success. How you treat them at the first crusade will determine what level of involvement they will have if you ever return for another crusade.

III.13.1.1.2. Prayer Support

Do not overlook the benefits, power and purpose of prayer when making plans for the crusade. Get the local churches praying long before you arrive. Establish prayer committees who will coordinate 24-hour prayer chains and prayer vigils. Enlist the help of local prayer warriors who will commit to time in prayer for the success of the crusade. Each person who is involved in the crusade should be willing to undergird all of the efforts and plans with intense prayer and that prayer should be specific in focus. Intercede in prayer on behalf of every aspect of the crusade.

First, pray for every worker. If you can't call them by individual name, pray for them by assigned responsibility. Pray for those who will be handling publicity. Pray for those who will be providing crowd control (ushers, etc.). Pray for the church leaders that their congregations will catch the vision and importance of the crusade. Provide as much prayer support for everyone involved as possible. Do not be lulled into a false sense of security by thinking if you have an abundance of workers you don't have to worry about satanic attacks. Use a leap of intelligence and pray for individual personal needs, health, safety and strength in areas of personal weakness. Satan will attack your leadership first. Pray for harmony of vision and purpose. If Satan can bring division or strife within the leadership, he won't have to worry about the event itself. Know this ... as your team strives to prepare and draw closer to the Lord, satanic attacks will come, will come often, and will come with intensity.

Pray for the hearts and souls of the unbelievers who will attend. Pray for a harvest. If you're not concerned about the souls, why are you conducting the crusade? Check your motives. Pray that the Lord will quicken the hearts of the masses, that he will open their ears to hear his Word. Pray that the message you deliver will be from God, anointed by his Holy Spirit and empowered to do his work. Pray for these people long before the crusade begins. Pray for them during the crusade. Pray for them after the crusade. Before the crusade they will need the quickening of the Holy Spirit to attend. During the crusade they will need the convicting power of the Holy Spirit to bring them to a saving knowledge of Jesus Christ. After the crusade they will need the strength of the Holy Spirit to stand and grow in their new faith. Be specific in your prayers. Ask God for specific numbers of salvations and healings. Be realistic, however. If the community only has a few hundred people, it might be unrealistic to ask for thousands. Nevertheless, ask for God's blessings and anointing, trusting him to bring everything to pass.

Pray against the enemy. This is not just praying for the workers or for the new converts. This is praying against the satanic or demonic strongholds in the community. It may be witchcraft, demonology or even the lust for power, success and money. Whatever satanic activity is prevalent in the community must be confronted and torn down. You may not even be aware of what they are. Ask the Holy Spirit to reveal them to you. Seek the godly wisdom of the local leadership as to how you should pray. Enlist your prayer warriors and prayer committee to be specific in their stand against satanic influences. This is warfare. This is a battle. Just as you are praying for the people, pray against Satan. Bind him, in Jesus' name. Rebuke his efforts. You have the power and authority of Almighty God on your side. Satan will not let your plans go forth without a fight. Tear down the strongholds. *"For the weapons of our warfare are not carnal, but mighty through God to the pulling down of strong holds"* (2 Corinthians 10:4). This is your promise from God. Use it. Stand on it. Be bold.

Additional Reading

Read from *Evangelism By Fire*
chapter 20 on pages 187-197
Faith – The Link With God's Power
chapter 21 on pages 102-108
of the book passage compilation

Module III
Lesson 14
Principles of Global Evangelism (continued)

III.14.1. Preaching Crusades (continued)

III.14.1.1. Preparing through Administration

III.14.1.1.1. Committees

In Exodus 18, Moses' father-in-law, Jethro, saw that the load Moses was carrying was too much for one person. Moses was trying to do everything to take care of the children of Israel. This was too much. Jethro counseled Moses that he needed to divide the labor among others. Moses could not be all things to all people. *"Thou wilt surely wear away, both thou, and this people that is with thee: for this thing is too heavy for thee; thou are not able to perform it thyself alone"* (Exodus 18:18). This was wise counsel.

The same could be said about the evangelist who thinks he has to do everything in planning and preparation for the crusade. It's unrealistic to think that. It could even be considered self-serving and vain. The evangelist who tries to do everything will inevitably forfeit time that he needs in spiritual preparation for the crusade itself. So, as Jethro counseled Moses to delegate authority and establish a chain of command, the evangelist should heed similar counsel and establish leadership and committees that can focus on specific needs for the crusade.

Publicity: Whatever the venue, you will need some form of publicity or getting the word out about the crusade. This might be so involved as to include television, radio and newspaper advertisements or it might be as simple as printing small fliers for personal distribution and/or word of mouth. This committee should determine every means that is feasible and affordable for publicizing the event. The committee should start its planning early and provide ample publicity leading up to the crusade. Make sure the publicity has all of the important information that someone would need to know (what, where, when). The publicity campaign might start simply at first with spot announcements or fliers. Then, as the crusade draws closer, the intensity of the publicity should be increased. Don't forget that during the crusade, publicity needs to continue.

Safety / Security / Crowd Control: The size of the venue will determine how big your crowds can be. It is better to plan for too many than to not be prepared. Determine how people will access the venue. Look for possible danger areas (areas where people could injure themselves or areas where it would be difficult for the people to move easily). If the venue will have parking availability, determine how that will be handled. It might be that you will want to have several subcommittees that focus on some of these key areas (e.g., Traffic Committee, Usher Committee, etc.). What will you do about seating? You might include in this restroom accessibility and first aid availability. The committee needs to make sure they have planned for every reasonable possibility. There will always be things that you might not think about, but if you have tried to look at every aspect and have planned accordingly, you will minimize the potential for accidents and your own liability.

Altar and Prayer Counselors: In addition to the prayer support that must occur prior to the crusade, there should be training for workers who will be assisting in the altar times. Your altar workers and prayer counselors should be well-versed in scripture and have sound biblical theology. The local churches are good sources for these individuals. The counselors should be trained in how to pray with people, how to counsel people, and how to make referrals for individuals whose needs are beyond their expertise and/or capabilities. If you are planning to have a healing crusade, have medical personnel available to document the healings and provide medical assistance when needed. Training sessions should be planned well ahead of the crusade so your workers will have confidence in what they will be called upon to do. This committee will also need to be able to work closely with the ushers to control crowd movement during the altar service. A subcommittee of this might also be one that oversees a prayer room (or tent) for on-going prayer and/or counseling during the crusade. Cover the event with prayer at all times.

Finances: The evangelist should not be the one directly involved with the financial accounting. There should be a committee with no one person having sole oversight. This serves as a checks and balances for financial accountability. Keep clear records. Account for every offering, every gift ... account for every expenditure. You must have accurate and fiscally sound accounting of all monies that are handled. The committee should make sure all bills are paid. Financial misappropriation is one of the easiest areas for satanic attack. Make sure that doesn't happen. Have honest, responsible individuals in charge of this area, individuals who understand accounting and who will keep good records. Note every expenditure. Get receipts. If receipts are not available, make notes of every detail related to money coming in and money being spent. You can have volunteers to count the offerings, but you need people who have a knowledge of accounting to oversee the financial records. Do not place the sole responsibility for this on only one individual.

There are numerous other committees that can be established, depending on the type of crusade. If there are to be children or youth activities, there will need to be a committee to oversee those events. If there are book/tape products for sale, there will need to be a committee to oversee that. What about refreshments and water? If you are going to have that available, someone will have to coordinate the vendors.

The committees don't have to be large ... they just have to be adequate to make sure every aspect of the crusade is handled properly. The evangelist would probably want to have a steering committee that will have oversight of the other committees. He could work more closely with that committee and let the other committees function without his direct supervision. Keep a chain of command. Keep accountability. Above all, keep all committees (and volunteers) focused on the purpose of the crusade. Each committee's function is important to the success of the campaign and none should be considered of lesser importance.

III.14.1.1.2. Venue

Visit the venue site early. Do a thorough analysis of the strengths and weaknesses of the venue and also of any problem areas. Visit the venue at the time of day when the crusade will be occurring to determine traffic patterns. Is it large enough to accommodate the anticipated crowd? Does it have sufficient space for what you want to do during the crusade? What will you do for overflow? Notice the types of facilities and equipment that are available. What is already there? What will you have to bring in yourself? Is electricity available? Is the area secure? Are there facility rental contracts that have to be completed? What kind of government license or permit do you need? Are there fees to pay? Look at the venue with a critical eye to see what you will have and what you will need. Then, plan your crusade budget accordingly.

III.14.1.1.3. Equipment

Your equipment needs will be determined by the type of program you are planning during the crusade and the type of venue you will be using. Your sound system should be adequate to reach all areas of the venue. Will the crusade be televised? Will there be visual enhancement through large screen projection? Are there drama presentations? What will be the music needs? If the crusade is at night, what will be the lighting needs? If taking up an offering, what will be needed to accommodate the crowds (i.e., offering plates, bags, buckets, etc.) Whatever is required for these must be determined and provided for. Will the equipment be brought in, rented, or borrowed? Where will the equipment be stored during the day? What kind of security will you have for keeping the equipment safe? Who will be responsible for running or using the equipment? How will you keep account of the equipment during the crusade? These are details that the evangelist does not need to be concerned with; however, he will need to have someone who will shoulder that responsibility, either individually or through committee.

III.14.1.1.4. Set-Up / Tear-Down

Once you have determined the venue and have determined what your specific needs will be, it becomes necessary to plan for setting up the venue, manning it daily, and tearing down the equipment after the crusade. There is usually excitement and no shortage of volunteers before the crusade begins so set-up is probably not going to be a problem. You will simply need someone to coordinate everything, making sure each piece of equipment is in its proper place prior to the start of the first service. If plans are not made for sufficient personnel to take care of tearing down the equipment after the crusade is over, that can become an overwhelming task for the faithful few who remain. Therefore, it is essential to have a post-crusade plan in place with adequate personnel to take care of collecting all the equipment, making sure it is returned to the appropriate place(s), and cleaning up the venue. If the venue is rented, there will probably be contractual requirements about how the venue is to be left.
If there is no contract, it is unacceptable for the evangelistic team to leave the venue dirty and in disarray. *"... whatsoever ye would that men should do to you, do ye even so to them ..."* (Matthew 7:12). In other words, leave the venue the way you would want it left for you.

III.14.1.1.5. Budget

You've visited the site. You've analyzed your equipment needs. You've noted the other expenses involved in setting up and tearing down. All of that is inconsequential if you haven't considered your budget for the crusade. How will the crusade be funded? If you are funding it entirely on contributions, what assurance do you have that there will be sufficient monies to cover the expenses. There are some expenses that can possibly be delayed; there are some expenses that will require immediate payment. Planning a budget is not a lack of faith in God's ability to provide. Rather, it's demonstrating good stewardship of the financial resources available. Yes, God can provide for every need. That is not a license for extravagant overspending. Establish a budget and stay within the budget. Pay all vendors in a timely manner. You may be operating as a ministry of faith but your vendors may not be. Most importantly, as mentioned previously, set a means of financial accountability. Keep records of all income and expenses and make sure you have more than one person with this responsibility.

Additional Reading

**Reread from *Evangelism By Fire*
chapter 17 on pages 163-171 of the book passage compilation**

III.14.1.1.6. Planning Meetings

Your committees will have responsibility for their areas of focus. Meet with the committee leadership early in the planning process so each committee has a clear understanding of their responsibilities and the responsibilities of the other committees. Look for overlaps and look for areas that have been overlooked. Pray with the leadership ... pray for God's anointing and for God's wisdom in the details. Meet regularly for progress updates. Have planning sessions to evaluate where you are in the plans and what else needs to be done. Have someone revisit the venue to see if anything has been omitted. Do not rush these meetings. Allow time for sufficient planning. Give encouragement to your committee members and give recognition for the work they are doing. As with your church leadership, affirm your committee and crusade leadership. Each member is important and each member's role should not be taken for granted.

III.14.1.2.   Follow-Up

The crusade doesn't end when the last sermon is preached. Those who have been saved now must be nurtured, taught and discipled. For many of them, "salvation" is a foreign concept. They do not understand what has happened, nor do they grasp the impact this will have on their lives. They have been changed, forgiven, but they don't know what that means. The next step beyond the evangelistic crusade is the follow-up that must occur. As with the crusade, this requires planning and training.

III.14.1.2.1.   Records

Before the crusade, determine what kinds of information about new converts will be helpful to the local churches once the crusade is over. Create a form or some means of making a record of each convert's name, address, age, sex, and marital status – anything that would be good for the local church to know. This does not have to be an elaborate form. Find out what will work best for the local churches and use that. The different categories of information will help the local church know where the convert might have needs or interests. It would be good to keep duplicate records, if possible. That way the evangelist could have a record and the local church could have one.

III.14.1.2.2. Pastoral / Church Follow-Up and Discipleship

When meeting with the church leaders, establish a follow-up plan. How will the churches contact or follow-up with the new converts? How will you determine which churches get which names ... by geographical location, perhaps? Don't assume the new converts will automatically start going to church. As a parent looking after a small child, the new converts need similar guidance, if they are to grow in their relationship with the Lord. Make sure the churches are able to provide Bible-study and discipleship classes. The new converts should be contacted by the local churches as quickly as possible following the crusade. They will have to be encouraged to come to church. They may feel uncomfortable in a traditional church environment. Someone will have to reassure them, affirm them, encourage them, and, if necessary, walk with them through their growth process. The churches will have to welcome the new converts, overlooking their past mistakes and understanding their current misgivings, providing for them a safe haven in which they can grow without judgment or condemnation. If the churches are unwilling or unable to take the leadership role, individuals from the churches should be recruited who will assume the role of a spiritual parent. There must be follow-up if the new converts are to survive, for Satan will certainly do his part to try to challenge their new faith.

Module III
Lesson 15
Principles of Global Evangelism (continued)

Reference: *Time Is Running Out*

III.15.1.   Church Growth Evangelism

Everyone will not go to a foreign country to conduct large evangelistic crusades. All believers can, however, evangelize their communities. One of the most effective means of doing this is through church growth evangelism, i.e., using a visitation/ invitation campaign to bring non-churched individuals to the local church as a means of evangelistic outreach. As with the preaching crusades, prayer, planning, and perseverance can make the church growth evangelistic campaigns effective and productive. "Whatever particular forms your evangelism might take, unless you have some sort of plan, your impact will be lessened, or even lost" (*Time Is Running Out*).

III.15.1.1.   A Point of Contact

It is a lot easier to get non-churched people to attend a church service for a special event than it is to get them to attend for a regular worship service. The faithful members will come to services, no matter what; the non-churched (and/or less faithful) must have a special reason for coming. So, the local church can develop and promote key events that will draw people to the services. Then, once the people are there, the pastor and leadership can use the service as a means for evangelism. Never forget, as Evangelist Bonnke has stated, "Every method should be soul-winning and not just church-filling" (*Time Is Running Out*).

For example, non-churched people are often open to attending a special musical or dramatic event. Those same people might shy away from a traditional church worship service. Christmas musicals, Easter musicals/dramas, children's musicals, youth events, church auctions and festivals ... all of these can be extremely effective in bringing people to the church. Many churches have major productions that are used to draw in the community, all the while with the intent of presenting the gospel message as part of the production. It works!

So, if a church wants to put together a major evangelistic/church growth campaign, the leadership should first determine what type of presentation they want to prepare. This gives the church members a non-threatening event as a point of contact for the invitations they want to extend to their friends and families.

As with the preaching crusades, there needs to be a lot of prayer and planning for the event. Every detail should be considered so the event will go smoothly and the people who come will not be put off by poorly executed presentations. God expects us to give our best. That means everything we do should be done with the highest caliber of effort possible. That doesn't mean you have to put your church in debt to produce an event that is beyond your financial means. Budget, plan, and present a first-class event – within your financial capabilities or constraints. Cover the event planning and execution with prayer and, in faith, trust the Holy Spirit to quicken the hearts of those attending to receive the message.

Consider, for example, a special church dramatic production. This could be for a major service like Easter, or it could be a specialized event with no link to a particular Christian season. Once the event is determined, planning committees should be formed to delegate responsibilities to make sure every aspect of the successful completion of the event has been covered.

Committees, or individuals, should be recruited to oversee the many details. Your list of needs and concerns might include such things as:

1. **Coordination** – What type of planning or steering committee will need to be established? Who will be in charge? What is the line of accountability? This does not have to be a large group. There just needs to be some level of coordination of efforts and accountability.

2. **Spiritual Issues** – Will there be a need for prayer teams, altar workers, counselors? Who will train them and coordinate their tasks? Don't leave God out of the planning!

3. **Publicity** – How will you publicize the event? Will you use radio/television advertisements? Are there free public service announcement spots available? Will you put ads in the local newspapers? Will there be publicity fliers printed? How will those be distributed? Will this be a ticketed event? If you don't publicize in some fashion, you probably will not get the attendance response you want. Your church membership will come, but others might not.

4. **Budget** – What type of budget has been set aside for the event? How will the event be funded? Will you sell tickets? Will you take up an offering? (Don't do both.) What will be the expenses? Overspending and under-budgeting can wreck a local congregation. Be financially accountable and good stewards of the financial resources the Lord has provided for the local church.

5. **Production Issues** – Will you need to construct some type of set? How many workers are needed to do that? Will you need to secure or make props? Will you rent or make your own costumes? Who will take care of the costuming needs? Are there other equipment needs, e.g., lighting, sound, etc.? Who will be responsible for tearing down the set, collecting the props and costumes, and returning borrowed or rented items after the production? The behind-the-scenes work is crucial for the success of the production. Get people who know what they are doing to oversee the technical aspects.

6. **Rehearsals** – If this is a musical or dramatic presentation, who is in charge? How will you cast the presentation? When will you have rehearsals? Have you made sure the rehearsals and performances do not conflict with other church (or even major civic) events? Sometimes the musical director and drama director are two different people. They must be able to coordinate their efforts and respect each other's expertise.

7. **Volunteers** – What kind and number of volunteers do you need? How will you recruit them? Who will coordinate their efforts? Will you need people for ushers? Will you need people for traffic control and parking? You will need volunteers for every aspect. Love on them. Affirm them. Appreciate them. They are the backbone of your church.

8. **Security** – What type of security will be needed? Anticipate the needs and be prepared. It is better to be prepared.

9. **Nursery** – Will there be a nursery available for infants and small children? Who will coordinate the workers for the nursery? Will those workers be paid? If the event is for only one night, volunteers may be hard to recruit since most of your people will want to attend the production. If you pay nursery workers, be sure to include the salaries in your overall budget.

10. **Follow-up** – How will follow-up be handled? Are there sufficient classes or groups to accommodate the new converts? Your purpose for the church growth evangelistic campaign should be focused on how to minister to and evangelize those who attend. All else is secondary!

This seems like a lot of effort for a local church production, but all of these types of issues (and more) need to be considered for the production to go smoothly and to be the most effective. The depth of planning and the expense involved will be significantly less than that required for a preaching crusade. Nevertheless, the details must be attended to and the view should not be that a local church campaign is of less importance or less value than a large preaching crusade.

III.15.1.2. Training for Grassroots Campaigns

In addition to the planning, there should be training provided for the participants. Many lay members of a local church may already be skilled at inviting people to church. Others may not be comfortable with doing so, quite possibly because they just do not know how to do it. Local churches can provide seminars, courses and conferences on how to evangelize, soul-winning, and how to invite people. The decision to do so is up to the leadership of the church.

First, and foremost, the leadership of the church should help instill in the congregation a love of the lost and a passion for seeing them saved. The church should be led into a realization that soul-winning is not just the role of the pastor or church leadership. Rather, every person who wears the title of Christian should be enveloped by the desire to see others brought to Christ. The Great Commission is for everyone, not just the church leadership.

It's easy to love those who are like us. It's not so easy to love those who are different. The Bible doesn't make a distinction. The Father loved us while we were sinners and sent his son to be the propitiation for our sins. If he who was perfect had love that great for us, the unredeemed, how much more should we love those who are as we once were. We are told that God is love. God's love transcends all barriers and we can do no less than to share that love with those who do not know him.

The church, the members of the church, must recognize their own sinful nature and the plight of those who are lost. In so doing, they cannot help but have compassion for those who are dying in sin. Let love be your motivation. Let salvation of the lost be your goal.

Additional Reading

Read from *Time Is Running Out*
chapter 7 on pages 17-28 of the book passage compilation

III.15.1.3. Specialized Evangelism and Annual Events

In addition to major events, the church can also offer programs that
are age or gender specific that will appeal to the membership and
will also open doors for non-believers. These would include programs
specifically for children (e.g., Vacation Bible School, camps), youth
(e.g., retreats, camps, activity nights, coffee houses), singles (e.g., Bible
studies, recreational events), married couples (e.g., home fellowship
groups, social gatherings, parenting seminars), senior citizens
(e.g., trips, dinners), men (e.g., retreats, sports outings) and women
(e.g., Bible study teas, gender-specific seminars, craft programs).
Of course, many of the examples given could be used for any age
or gender group. All of those listed are non-threatening and more
relaxed programs that might appeal to people outside the church. Be
creative. These types of programs are excellent vehicles for bringing
people into fellowship within the church. In all things, the goal for
the unbeliever is salvation. Use these specialized types of events as
evangelistic outreaches. They can be very effective.

You may not see great results from a single event. The consistency
of multiple events for a group will show the church's commitment
to the group (and to the individual). The more involved your people
become, the more likely they are to stay and commit. That's true with
non-believers. If they feel a connection to the group, they will be more
receptive to the message.

III.15.1.4. Training Lay Evangelists

An army of mice will get into places one elephant cannot enter.
The visual image of a group of mice scurrying in all directions is
evangelism at its best. Teach your laymen to be evangelists. Send them
forth as an army of mice, scattering to all corners of the community,
reaching areas where others might not think to go. Prepare them.
Teach them how to witness and how to lead someone in praying the
"sinner's prayer." Jesus spent three years training his disciples before

he sent them forth. They were inexperienced and not necessarily notable. Yet, their efforts revolutionized the world and introduced the Savior to all mankind. As a church, take action. Give your people the tools and weapons they need and then send them forth.

III.15.2. The Commission – Your Call

Evangelist Bonnke provides eight principles (keys) which lead to success, based on Joshua chapter one. The eighth principle is a call for "action" on the part of the believer.

> *Churches that act grow. Churches that simply sit looking at one another and dreaming, waiting for some special day, a revival day, praying for a different day, will eventually just die of old age. People who have done things to change the world did them when nobody thought it was the right time, when the advice was to wait for better conditions. But they acted and changed the conditions. That is how revival starts – somebody thinks they have prayed and waited long enough and gets on with the job of proclaiming the gospel.*

There are people who need to hear the message that you and your church can bring. How they respond is up to them; however, whether or not they are given an opportunity to respond is up to you. You have a call for action. If you don't tell them, who will?

Module IV
Lesson 16
The Ministry of the Word, Methods and Models of Discipleship and Follow-Up

Reference: *Mighty Manifestations*

There are basically three types of Word ministry: teaching, testimony and preaching. We will learn fundamentals of all three, practical structural form, and techniques to improve our ability to communicate and deliver in each of the forms. The crucial issue, however, is that the Bible is the authority. The ministry of the Word cannot be done with other writings that are apart from it or in contradiction to it. *"If any man shall add unto these things, God shall add unto him the plagues that are written in this book: And if any man shall take away from the words of the book of this prophecy, God shall take away his part out of the book of life, and out of the holy city, and from the things which are written in this book"* (Revelation 22:18-19).

IV.16.1. The Ministry of the Word

IV.16.1.1. Teaching

The critical aspects of teaching are information and illumination. The concept of teaching requires a more detailed approach that often deals with greater amounts of background and word study, emphasizing the depth of the text and the context in which it was written. Though all ministries have an evangelistic aspect, the teaching ministry is more of a focus to train and disciple through the Word.

In preparation for a teaching unit, the teacher must gain a clear understanding of the passage being taught. Ask yourself the following questions (or similar questions) about the passage and use the answers as the foundation for the lesson.

1. Who is talking?
2. To whom is that person talking?
3. What is the situation or circumstance surrounding this event?
4. What happened to cause this situation?
5. What is the result?
6. What is the real meaning of the text?
7. How does this apply to the lives of those being taught?
8. What are some key points in the passage?

Every text will not fit neatly into the pattern of these questions. The teacher will need to adapt the questions to fit the text. However, the preparation is the same, regardless of the text being taught. The teacher should find out the background and supporting circumstances of the text and use that foundationally to teach the key points. Often, an understanding of the background can enlighten the hidden meanings and enables the listener to better understand the emphasis of the lesson.

An Example:

Consider Acts 16:31: *"Believe on the Lord Jesus Christ, and thou shalt be saved, and thy house."* Using this verse as the foundation for the lesson, answer the questions based on the verses surrounding the key verse and then build on those answers to finalize the lesson.

1. Who is talking?
   Paul is speaking.

2. To whom is that person talking?
   Paul is speaking to the Philippian jailer.

3. What is the situation or circumstance surrounding this event?
   Paul and Silas have been miraculously delivered from prison.

4. What happened to cause this situation?
   Paul and Silas were arrested, beaten and imprisoned. While in prison they praised God in spite of their circumstances. An earthquake freed the prisoners and the jailer, believing the prisoners had escaped, feared for his own life.

5. What is the result?
   The jailer and his entire household were converted to faith in Jesus Christ.

6. What is the real meaning of the text?
   Faith in Jesus Christ can overcome circumstances and changes lives, eternities and entire families.

7. How does this apply to the lives of those being taught?
   Since God is no respecter of persons, all can be saved and find his blessings in their households. Additional subtexts might focus on the power of prayer and praise in all circumstances.

8. What are some key points in the passage?
a. *Persecution may pave the way to evangelism.* (Acts 16:19-24)
b. *The power of praise unlocks the supernatural, delivering power of God.*
   (Acts 16:25-26)
c. *Like Paul, we must be ready to love, forgive, and save those who have previously persecuted us.*
d. *Belief in Christ is enough to save the lost. Do not add burdens and complications on unbelievers.*
e. *When Jesus begins to move in a family, we can believe for all to be saved.*
f. *When the head of the household gets saved, it will be easier to reach the rest of the household.*

In addition to doing the necessary preparation for the lesson, the teacher should also consider how best to present the lesson. Traditional expository lectures, though often the easiest to prepare, are not always the best vehicle for delivery of the lesson. Educational theorists have long been proponents of the belief that the more involvement a student has in the lesson, the more likely that student is to retain its information and concepts. Turn your listeners into teachers through class or small group discussion. Develop key questions that will elicit responses from your students that will enhance the lesson. Many of your students may have insight into a passage that you might not have considered. The more involved they are, the less likely they are to daydream or think about other things.

Two cautions should be noted here. The teacher should maintain control of the discussion to make sure the students do not get caught up in discussing minutia and miss the primary objective of the lesson. Also, the teacher should guard against false doctrines or beliefs contrary to the Word that might arise during discussion times. Do not let the discussions get out of control or away from the purpose of the lesson.

When teaching, use examples to make or support your key points. Personal examples that illustrate the relevance of the passage are helpful in assisting the students in application of the passage to their own lives and circumstances. If they can grasp that the passage is more than a historical account or something that was only significant in Biblical times, they are more likely to see the implications of that passage for their own lives. Personal illustrations help them do that, helping them claim ownership of the message of the lesson.

Be mindful of the group you are teaching. Factors such as age, sex, marital status, educational and economic levels should be considered when preparing the lesson. For example, the age of the student certainly impacts the structure and the depth of the lesson. It would be unrealistic (and perhaps inappropriate) to expect lower elementary age students to understand certain aspects of the story of the woman caught in adultery (John 8:1-11). They can, however, grasp the key concepts of sin and forgiveness.

Consider, also, the historical and contextual realities of your own community (nation, city, village, or church). Cultural mores and/or biases should be considered for how the lesson could be applied to the lives of the students. A remote, rural village will not have the same perspectives on situations that might be found in metropolitan communities. That's not saying one environment is better than another; quite simply, it's just that one group's life experiences will not be the same as the other. In addition, recent political or social changes or upheavals should be considered in illustrating the relevance of passages.

Above all else, pray, study, and seek guidance from the Holy Spirit. God will hold you accountable for what you teach. *"You must teach what is in accord with sound doctrine"* (Titus 2:1, NIV). The Bible warns of false teachers and false doctrines and those who teach such will be judged accordingly (2 Peter 2). It is not a ministry that is to be taken lightly and the teacher should seek to present God's Word in fullness and without error.

Additional Reading

**Read from *Mighty Manifestations*
chapter 3 on pages 215-222 of the book passage compilation**

IV.16.1.2.   Testimony

The most informal and personal category of word ministry is testimony. Founded on personal experience, testimony presents the truth and power of God's actions in an individual's life. Testimony that violates scripture is not true testimony. Rather, testimony is tied to scripture by showing how promises God made in his word have been fulfilled in individual lives.

Testimonies can be powerful instruments for word ministry. Two of the best examples of the ministry and impact of testimony are given in the account of Peter's sermon at Pentecost (Acts 2) and Paul's trial before King Agrippa (Acts 26). Peter was empowered by the outpouring of the Holy Spirit and his sermon is a testimony of what the Lord had done. He did not take a passage of scripture and expound on it by teaching or preaching. He quite succinctly and powerfully testified about what had happened and used that testimony to proclaim the gospel, leading about 3,000 into a saving knowledge of Jesus Christ (Acts 2:41).

Similarly, when he was on trial before King Agrippa, Paul gave testimony of his conversion and the impact was so strong that he almost persuaded the pagan king to become a Christian (Acts 26:28). Though King Agrippa did not convert, the impact of Paul's testimony is, indeed, noteworthy and gives credence to the power of testimonial ministry.

A personal testimony does not require the depth of preparation that is necessary for a teaching or preaching ministry. There are times when testimony is spontaneous; however, when there is time to prepare, the testimony should be considered before being given. A simple outline can be followed. First, identify or explain a specific need in your life. Second, tell how the Lord met that need. Third, elaborate on the change that has occurred in your life and how your life is different now.

In John 9, there is the account of a man who had been blind from birth. Jesus healed the man. When the man was questioned by the Pharisees, he stated what was done and what happened. The Pharisees tried to press the man to declare that Jesus was a sinner for healing on the Sabbath. The man's response is a classic example of the simplicity of a true testimony. *"Whether he be a sinner or no, I know not: one thing I know, that, whereas I was blind, now I see"* (John 9:25).

This is testimony in its simplest form. The man did not try to give a great theological explanation of what had happened or its implications. He simply said, "I was blind, now I see." He had a need. Jesus met the need. His life was changed forever.

Testimonies can speak of conversion experiences such as the Saul's experience on the road to Damascus (Acts 9), healing or miracles such as the blind man (John 9), or spiritual progress through strength, patience, peace, etc.

Additional Reading

Read from *Mighty Manifestations*
***Three Pillars of Wisdom* on pages 201-202**
of the book passage compilation
Evangelist Reinhard Bonnke's personal testimony

IV.16.1.3. Preaching

Preaching must be first, and foremost, biblically based. In preparing a sermon, the evangelist should consider the same kinds of questions that were used for preparation of a teaching ministry. Determine the foundational aspects of the selected text. What was the purpose of the text? How can the text be applied to the life of the believer or in an evangelistic setting? Each text might have multiple themes. Do not feel you have to cover all of them. Choose one and focus on it, outlining your points from a biblical perspective and developing a theme to coordinate with them. In preparing, you must be careful that you don't read into the text something that it isn't saying. Consider the context in which the passage is found and the historical and cultural setting. That's why the foundational study is so critical; it helps the evangelist understand what is actually being said. Study and seek guidance from the Holy Spirit.

Paul challenged Timothy to *"study to shew thyself approved unto God ... rightly dividing the word by truth"* (2 Timothy 2:15) and to *"preach the word"* (2 Timothy 4:2). He encouraged Titus to *"speak thou the things which become sound doctrine"* (Titus 2:1). Anything that is preached which is contrary to the word of God is sin. God's judgment will fall on those who preach false doctrine. His word will not be compromised.

IV.16.1.3.1. Examples of Sermon Outlines

There are different types of sermons. 2 Timothy 3:16 states, *"All scripture is given by inspiration of God, and is profitable for doctrine, for reproof, for correction, for instruction in righteousness."* The focus of your sermon, whether it is evangelistic, admonishing, instruction, will be determined, in part, by the makeup of the group to which you are preaching. Let us consider a sermon that might be used as a teaching or instructing sermon on obedience, with Acts 8:25-40 as the text.

> **Text:**   Acts 8:25-40
> **Title:**   The Obedient Evangelist
> **Theme:** Obedience

An outline for this sermon might look like this:

I. Unquestioning Obedience (Acts 8:27a)

"... and he arose and went."

The focus here might be Philip's willingness to do what he was told without question. He was told to "go toward the south ..." and he did that. He left a busy city area (reference the verses prior to this passage) and went to a desert area. He had no idea why he was to go. Human nature would have wanted to know why but he didn't question the wisdom of going. He didn't try to come up with excuses for not going. He was told to go; he went.

II. Eager Obedience (Acts 8:30a)

"And Philip ran ..."

When instructed to go to the Ethiopian eunuch's chariot, Philip ran. The fact that Luke (the writer of Acts) specifically noted that Philip ran gives testimony to the fact that Philip was a willing and eager servant of God. The eunuch was a man of great authority, the treasurer for Candace, the Ethiopian queen (v. 27). Philip didn't know him and, quite possibly, may have felt out of place approaching someone of this position. Yet, when told to go to the eunuch, Philip ran. Not knowing what he was to do nor what he was to say, Philip still ran. His eagerness to be obedient overshadowed any hesitancies or questions he might have had.

III. Wise Obedience (Acts 8:35)

"Then Philip opened his mouth, and began at the same scripture, and preached unto him Jesus."

Unquestioning in his obedience to God and eager to do the work the Lord had placed before him, Philip wisely recognized this propitious moment and seized the opportunity to witness to and instruct the eunuch in the prophecies of Isaiah and their fulfillment in Jesus Christ. With wisdom and boldness, under the empowerment and guidance of the Holy Spirit, Philip turned a chance encounter into an eternally life-changing moment for this man.

Many of the questions previously used in the discussion on teaching are applicable here, with some modifications. Considering these questions would form the foundation for your sermon. The obedience theme would be the direction you would follow in presenting the sermon, but the questions would serve as background and explanation for the circumstances surrounding the event and the significance of the event. With these questions in mind, you can take the theme of obedience and present how Philip's actions are applicable in the lives of believers today.

- Who are the central figures in the passage?
  Philip and the Ethiopian eunuch

- What is the situation or circumstance surrounding their encounter?
  Philip met the Ethiopian eunuch who was reading the writings of Isaiah. The eunuch did not understand what he was reading.

- What happened to cause this situation?
  An angel instructed Philip to go to the south. While there, Philip met the Ethiopian.

- What is the result?
  Philip explained the passage in Isaiah and preached to the eunuch that Jesus was the fulfillment of Isaiah's prophecy. The eunuch was saved and baptized.

- What is the meaning of the text?
  There are several themes that could be considered. For the purpose of this sermon, we would focus on Philip's obedience and the results of that obedience – the eunuch was saved.

- How does this apply to the lives of those being taught?
  God expects obedience. Obedience brings results.

- What are some key points in the passage?
  With the theme of obedience, emphasis would be given to the ways in which Philip was obedient and the fruit of that obedience.

The same passage can be outlined and preached in a multiplicity of ways without taking the passage out of context and without compromising its validity. A different theme focusing on the work and power of the Holy Spirit in evangelism might be developed as an inspirational message summoning evangelists to trust in the Holy Spirit for power, direction and anointing. This would be different from a teaching sermon in its approach and focus. It would still use the same passage. Its differing theme would not negate the integrity of the passage nor challenge the truths presented in the previous message.

Text: Acts 8:25-40
Title: The Holy Spirit is the Senior Evangelist
Theme: The Work and Power of the Holy Spirit
in Evangelism

An outline for this sermon might look like this:

I. The Holy Spirit knows where there are ready hearts.
(Acts 8:26,29)

"Go toward the south unto the way that goeth down from Jerusalem unto Gaza, which is desert" (v. 26)

"Go near, and join thyself to this chariot." (v. 29)

Philip was in Samaria when he was told to leave. He had no idea what he would encounter. The Holy Spirit knew exactly where the Ethiopian eunuch was, both physically and spiritually, and orchestrated an encounter that would reach a heart that was ripe for harvest.

II. The Holy Spirit grants faith for salvation as a work of grace.
(Acts 8:36-37)

"And the eunuch said, See here is water: what doth hinder me to be baptized? And Philip said, If thou believest with all thine heart, thou mayest. And he answered and said, I believe that Jesus Christ is the Son of God."

Philip was obedient. The eunuch's heart was ready to receive the message. The Holy Spirit granted the faith to receive salvation by believing and declaring that Jesus Christ is the Son of God. This was outside the scope of the eunuch's religious views. Only by Holy Spirit empowered faith could he believe and receive.

III. The Holy Spirit empowers, moves, and directs the evangelist
   (Acts 8:39)

"The Spirit of the Lord caught away Philip, that the eunuch saw him no more: and he went on his way rejoicing."

Philip was sent to the Ethiopian eunuch for a salvation encounter. When that was done, the Holy Spirit no longer needed Philip there. So, Philip was caught away for his next evangelistic mission, never to see the eunuch again. The work of the Holy Spirit was completed for this man and now the Holy Spirit led Philip to his next ministry opportunity.

The questions that we considered for the obedience sermon are also applicable and useful for this sermon, again, with modifications. The first few questions giving the principal participants and circumstances are the same. A different perspective might be considered for the following questions.

- What is the meaning of the text?
  For the purpose of this sermon, we would focus on the direction and power of the Holy Spirit in orchestrating a salvation encounter between Philip and the Ethiopian eunuch.

- How does this apply to the lives of those being taught?
  Our steps are guided by the Holy Spirit, not only for ministry but for salvation. The Holy Spirit takes an active part in our lives.

- What are some key points in the passage?
  Emphasis would be given to the ways the Holy Spirit knows our hearts, directs our steps and empowers us for ministry.

We have considered the same passage (Acts 8:25-40) from two different perspectives (obedience and the work of the Holy Spirit). In each sermon, the foundation of the message has been the same. Though different, the themes do not conflict with one another, but simply present an alternative view, applicable to the purpose for which the sermon has been developed. Are both sermons presenting biblical truths? To be sure! Are both sermons contextually accurate? Without a doubt! Does either sermon contradict the validity of the other? Absolutely not!

IV.16.1.3.2. Points of Access

Every sermon must have "points of access" or places where the message "comes alive" for the listener. That is, there must be in every sermon something that will connect with the listeners and draw them in to the message and its usefulness in their lives. Through the work of the Holy Spirit, some people will be reached in ways that the evangelist cannot anticipate. However, the evangelist should prepare the sermons (with prayer and study) in such a way that he incorporates opportunities where the sermon will provide those "points of access." In faith, the evangelist commits what he has prepared to the use of the Holy Spirit. The evangelist is the vehicle; the message, through the Holy Spirit, is the cargo that will reach the heart of the listener.

There are two kinds of "points of access." Illustrations make the points of the message clear to the listener. Applications make the points of the message personal.

IV.16.1.3.2.1. Illustrations

Illustrations do not need to be deep in theological perspective. Quite the contrary, they should be kept simple, easily understood by the listener. The purpose of the illustration is to take a major point in the sermon and provide an example or story that emphasizes that one point. The illustration should be culturally relevant, something to which the listeners can relate. One illustration per major point should be sufficient. If you try to give two many illustrations to emphasize a point, you run the risk of confusing the point you are trying to make. The source of illustrations is limitless. They can come from literature, real life, the Bible, current events, cultural folklore, historical events, and any other source that illustrates the lesson being taught. The key is they should illustrate succinctly the major point and not detract from it.

The parables that Jesus used were illustrations which the people could understand. Jesus was an extremely gifted teacher. He knew how to make his points and then emphasize the points by illustrations that related to the people where they were. He used everyday, common experiences to connect with the people at a level they could understand.

IV.16.1.3.2.2. Applications

A major component of any sermon is the time where the message or meaning of the sermon is made applicable to the listeners. If they do not grasp how the message is important in their lives, its relevancy, the delivery of the sermon is in vain. They will simply go away thinking it was a nice message but doesn't relate to them. After you have made your points, given the illustrations, you then must take the key points and summarize them in a way that shows the relevancy of the message to each individual.

In other words, you must reach a point in the sermon when you can either say verbally or imply, "This is what it means to married couples, to youth, or to whatever group of people to whom you are ministering."

If you were preaching a sermon on John the Baptist, you might use his lifestyle in the desert (Matthew 3:1-4) as an application of the sacrifices that others do for their jobs, e.g., soldiers who don't complain about the conditions in which they have to work. The essence of the application is that you are giving the listeners something to grasp that will instill in them the meaning of the message and its implication for their lives.

IV.16.1.3.3. Invitation

The culmination of the message (sermon, illustrations and applications) is the invitation. This is what you are moving toward, inviting others to repent and believe on the Lord Jesus Christ. This is the ultimate goal of the evangelistic sermon. As such, it is essential that the invitation be ...

1. Clear

Do not confuse the congregation. Make the invitation to repent clear and succinct. You do not need to cloud the issue with flowery words. If you have presented your sermon well, the congregation will understand that what you are asking them to do is really quite simple – repent and believe. Tell the people the only way of salvation is through Jesus Christ. Nothing else they can do is sufficient. Many will fear there is more they have to do, that this is too simple; assure them of God's forgiveness – repent and believe.

2. Authoritative

Your authority for the requirements – and promises – of salvation is scripture. You do not have to fear. You do not have to doubt. You do not have to apologize. Present God's Word ... let the Holy Spirit do the rest. You do not have to whitewash the gospel. Repent and believe. As one anointed to deliver the message of God's salvation, take authority over Satan and proclaim that there is no other way except through Jesus Christ. That way is all they need.

3. Loving

More than anything else, people want to be loved. Many may doubt their worthiness. Truly, no one is worthy to receive God's love and forgiveness of sins. Nevertheless, God looks beyond our unworthiness and offers a means whereby we can be saved. As you extend the invitation, show the same love that was shown to you. Do not judge the individual for who he is, what he looks like or where he has been. Look upon these immortal men through the eyes of an immortal God. His concern is not where they have come from; rather, his concern is where they are going and what they will decide today. You can offer nothing less. Do not be argumentative. Let the people see your love, compassion, and concern for their eternal salvation.

4. Genuine

Let your love and compassion for the lost be genuine. This is no time for you to put on a fake smile and disingenuous concern. Be sincere. If you don't have a passion for the lost, ask God to give you that burden. If those to whom you are ministering do not feel you are genuinely concerned about them, they are not likely to respond to your invitation. Conversely, if they feel your invitation is given out of genuine love and compassion, they will appreciate what you say and will be open to respond.

IV.16.2. Methods and Models of Discipleship and Follow-Up

IV.16.2.1. Discipleship

"And Jesus came and spake unto them, saying, 'All power is given unto me in heaven and in earth. Go ye therefore, and teach all nations, baptizing them in the name of the Father, and of the Son, and of the Holy Ghost: Teaching them to observe all things whatsoever I have commanded you: and, lo, I am with you always, even unto the end of the world." (Matthew 28:18-20). The moment of salvation is real and profound, yet the work of "making disciples" has, at that point, only begun.

"Our mission is to bring power. That is all we are – just power men, laying the power lines into powerless lives ... The Great Commission has its own in-built power source. The Holy Spirit is bound to honour the Gospel. It burns with power. You can no more carry it out without power than carry fire without heat. The Great Commission and power are not loosely connected – they are mutually dependent. If we go, He goes. If we work, He works." God provides the power. We, then, bring the power through evangelism and through our prayerful commitment to God, realizing that He is the source of our power.

The Great Commission is not just about evangelism, however. Look again at a portion of the passage quoted earlier: *"Go ye therefore, and teach all nations ... teaching them to observe all things whatsoever I have commanded you ..."* (Matthew 28:19-20). Too often Christians equate the Great Commission as being totally about evangelism. It is not. Evangelism is not just about proclaiming the gospel. That's only the first step. Beyond the initial impact of salvation, there is a great need for new believers to be discipled in their faith. Evangelism is, certainly, the key initial element, but there also has to be a plan of discipleship, whereby the new converts are taught and nurtured as they grow in their relationship with the Savior. One cannot assume their new birth has ushered them into full maturity of faith and knowledge. To lead someone into salvation and then leave him to survive on his own is a travesty. There must be a time for teaching and growth, in order for them to become mature Christians. Discipleship is a key element of evangelism, for it is through discipleship that the new convert receives instruction and, ultimately, is able to grasp the power that belongs to all believers. Through discipleship, the weak are made strong and are able to continue to fulfill the commission given to all ... go and preach. Let's briefly consider two examples of discipleship (Paul and Timothy; Jesus and his disciples).

IV.16.2.1.1. Paul and Timothy

Paul first met Timothy at Lystra (Acts 16:1) and because he was well reported, Timothy was invited to join Paul in ministry (Acts 16:3-5). Timothy was young in the faith and Paul worked with him so that he (Timothy) could grow in his relationship with the Lord and could become the mighty man of God which he was ordained to be. Timothy

became Paul's spiritual child and, in time, eventually became the
apostle's associate and representative. Timothy demonstrated the
kind of qualities that Paul respected and Paul took leadership in
training and discipling Timothy. As Timothy matured, Paul more
and more trusted him and placed him in positions of authority
and responsibility. (1 Thessalonians 3:1-5, 1 Corinthians 4:17,
1 Timothy 1:3). Paul's counsel to Timothy is presented in two letters,
written while Timothy was laboring among the believers at Ephesus.
Timothy's spiritual growth and maturity is evident in the writings
of Paul and Paul's confidence and affection for this "spiritual son" is
well-documented.

Timothy was an outstanding young man. But he did not spring forth
a mature believer. Inevitably, he stumbled, made bad decisions,
and, perhaps, even questioned his faith. However, Paul's love and
nurturing helped Timothy to overcome whatever obstacles he may
have faced and empowered him to serve God to his fullest. Would
he have been as successful in ministry without Paul's instruction?
Perhaps, but we will never know the answer to that. Nevertheless,
we know that Paul took special effort to nurture and teach Timothy
and the wisdom of Paul's counsel and discipling serves as a model for
pastors and mentors today.

IV.16.2.1.2. Jesus and His Disciples

Truly, there is no greater example of discipleship than that
demonstrated by Jesus Christ and his disciples. Jesus' example with
his disciples epitomizes discipleship at its best. For three years
of ministry, Jesus poured into the twelve the very wisdom and
instruction of God. He taught them, he led by example, he nurtured
them, knowing there would come a time when he would no longer be
with them and they would have to stand firm on the foundation that
he established in them.

There was no greater teacher, no greater example, no greater mentor.
All that the disciples became was a direct result of the impact Jesus

had on their lives. Though he taught the masses, his most intense times of discipleship occurred during those intimate moments that he shared with the twelve. The disciples of Christ saw first hand the gospel at the height of its power and strength. They witnessed the miracles of Christ and were privy to his deepest teachings. He used simple illustrations to present complex spiritual truths, leading his disciples to a deeper understanding of who they were and what they were called to be.

He revealed the hidden mysteries of heaven in language the disciples could understand and when he left them, he commissioned them to take that which they had received and change the world. When it was time for them to lead, they were ready. They knew the Savior of whom they spoke and they could testify to his works and ministry.

Why did Paul spend so much time with Timothy? Why was Jesus so longsuffering and patient with the disciples? Why should we be concerned about the spiritual growth of new believers? Paul clearly answers that in Ephesians 4:12-13 (NIV) when he writes, *"to prepare God's people for works of service, so that the body of Christ may be built up until we all reach unity in the faith and in the knowledge of the Son of God and become mature, attaining to the whole measure of the fullness of Christ."*

Look at parts of that passage again. What is the purpose of discipleship?

1. To prepare God's people for works of service
2. To build up the body of Christ
3. To help the body reach unity in faith and knowledge
4. To lead others into maturity

IV.16.2.1.3. To Prepare God's People for Works of Service

The Great Commission is a command – "Go!" We would not entrust a young driver with the keys to a new car without first making sure the driver was tested, trained and, in every way, equipped for whatever might come his way while driving the car. Jesus had tested, trained and, in every way, equipped his disciples for whatever might come their way while they were fulfilling the Great Commission. So it is with believers today. Our call is first to evangelize. Then, we are to prepare the new believers so they can do the works of service for which they have been called.

IV.16.2.1.4. To Build Up the Body of Christ

Believers do not exist in individual vacuums. We are all part of the body of Christ and each has an important part to play in the ministry of that body. No one is of lesser importance than another. However, the Church will only be as strong as its weakest member. Therefore, another purpose of discipleship is to build up the individual members of the body. As you strengthen the individual, the Church as a unit becomes stronger.

IV.16.2.1.5. To Help the Body Reach Unity in Faith and Knowledge

As the body becomes stronger, each member comes to an understanding of the place and importance of the other members. That harmony of focus brings about a unity of purpose and a unity of faith. Additionally, each believer brings insight into the gospel and where one's knowledge may be weak, another's may be strong.

IV.16.2.1.6. To Lead Others into Maturity

God does not want us to stay as infant believers. He expects us to grow. Children are cute and lovable, but God's plan for humanity is not that we stay as children. The natural process of life is growth and maturity. Nothing stays in its infant stage. With maturity comes the ability to work, to minister ... to evangelize. Mature Christians are grounded in the Word, empowered by the Holy Spirit, strong in their faith, energetic in their purpose, and dedicated to a life of service. Mature Christians are the spiritual adults God intended for them to be.

IV.16.2.2. The Body

"For we are his workmanship, created in Christ Jesus unto good works, which God hath before ordained that we should walk in them" (Ephesians 2:10). You are God's special creation, created to be a specific kind of person, created to do a specific kind of work, created to impact the world in a specific kind of way. As believers, it is our responsibility to find out who we are and where we fit into the body of Christ. Until he returns, we are the living, breathing, tangible embodiment of God. Others may be like you in many ways, but no one (not even an identical twin) is exactly like you in every way. If God made you specifically unique, surely there is a purpose for your life that only you can fulfill. If you fail to accept the responsibility, God will call someone else to do the work, but that person will be a secondary choice, bridging the gap that is made by your non-acceptance of your divinely ordained role, but not fulfilling the role as adequately as you would be able to do.

IV.16.2.3. Personal Growth

You cannot lead others to find their place in the body of Christ, if you are uncertain about yours or uncommitted to what God has for you. The steps you take to grow in your personal maturity parallel the steps that should be taken by every new believer. Each of us should not only instruct new believers in how to grow in their faith, knowledge and understanding, but we should model for them those things that they can do. There is an old adage that states, "Practice what you preach." In other words, if you are going to be instrumental in helping new believers grow, don't just tell them ... show them. If you tell them to pray, you should be praying. If you tell them to read their Bible, you should be reading your Bible. Be an example for them to follow. Then, they will have a better understanding of what they should be doing.

Consider Ezra 7:10, *"For Ezra had prepared his heart to seek the law of the Lord, and to do it, and to teach in Israel statutes and judgments."* Ezra prepared himself first; then he taught others. He decided he would study the scriptures and obey God's law. Then he was able to teach God's laws to the Israelites. This should be your perspective in your preparation. Your personal study and spiritual growth are not solely for your benefit. As you grow, you are able to help others in their growth, discipling them so they, in turn can disciple others. Your growth brings about their growth which brings about the growth of the body of Christ.

IV.16.2.3.1. Bible Study

When you want to know someone, you strive to find out all you can about that individual. Bible study is the believer's most revealing passage into the mind of God. It provides God's plan for every area of life and is fully inspired by God (2 Timothy 3:16). When you consider that the Bible was written by many different people, over many centuries, in three different languages and yet still has one central thread that is consistent throughout all of the writings, one can only conclude that this is truly the Holy Spirit inspired, infallible word of God. In Ephesians 6:17 it is referred to as the "sword of the Spirit." Armed with this sword, you not only come to a better understanding of the nature of God, you are also empowered to withstand and fight against the attacks of the enemy. Jesus himself used Old Testament scriptures to repel the temptations of Satan during the wilderness experience. (Luke 4) If Satan was bold enough to try to tempt the very Son of God, do not be so naïve as to think he will leave you alone. The Word of God is one of your weapons of warfare. It makes you strong. Satan may try to argue with you, but he cannot argue against the Word of God. It is your spiritual food. It guides you, enlightens you, and is your source of strength and power. The daily practical application of God's Word in your life is the foundation on which your ministry will stand. Know it. Use it. Rely on it.

IV.16.2.3.2. Meditation on the Word of God

Read Romans 12:1-5. You'll never find your place in the body of Christ if you are trying to hold onto a worldly life style. Paul tells us to "renew" our minds so that we can *"prove what is that good, and acceptable, and perfect will of God"* (v. 2). Meditation is prayerful reflection with an intent to gain insight, understanding of purpose and relevance. Meditation goes hand-in-hand with Bible study. Through meditation, the believer strives to conform to the will of God through reflection and thought on God's Word and its application to his own life. This is not to be confused with transcendental meditation or new age thought practices. The source and focus of your meditation should be the Bible, the laws of God and their application to your life. (Philippians 4:8)

IV.16.2.3.3. Prayer

Prayer is your communication with God. Too often we see prayer as only a time for asking God for specific needs or desires. That is a very minor facet of prayer. Jesus knew the importance of prayer and continually sought time with the Father (Mark 1:35). To grow in your spiritual walk, prayer, time spent in intimate communion with the Father, is essential. Through prayer you enter the throne room of God, finding mercy and grace in time of need (Hebrews 4:16). God is not a great philanthropist, casting gifts and rewards to all who cry out. He promises to answer our prayers, if we abide in him. *"If you abide in me, and my words abide in you, then you shall ask what you will, and it shall be done unto you"* (John 15:7). The key is where we are in Christ. If we are growing and maturing, our desires will be in alignment with God's purpose for our lives. As a believer, prayer should be an integral part of your daily walk. Nevertheless, it is an area that is easily forsaken or given a low priority.

Jesus gave us the perfect example of prayer when he taught his disciples how to pray (Matthew 6:9-15, Luke 11:1-4). Meditate on the Lord's Prayer (Matthew 6:9-15) and use it as a pattern for your prayers.

What better model to follow than the one presented by the Son of God! God desires to spend time with his children. His children need to spend time with their Father.

IV.16.2.3.4. Church Involvement and Fellowship with Believers

"And let us consider one another to provoke unto love and to good works: Not forsaking the assembling of ourselves together, as the manner of some is; but exhorting one another." (Hebrews 10:24-25)

Jesus established the church when he made his declaration to Peter, *"... upon this rock I will build my church; and the gates of hell shall not prevail against it"* (Matthew 16:18). The early Christians found strength from one another through the fellowship of the church. The church was given the responsibility to take care of the widows and children.

The church has the responsibility to be the spiritual family to the believer. Just as we need our parents and families to care for us and to protect us. The church serves as the family that cares for its members, protecting them, loving them, and even correcting them when they make mistakes. The fellowship of the believers, either through the local church or fellowship group, is crucial for the spiritual well-being of the believer. The church (i.e., the members) serves as accountability group, holding each member responsible for his actions and personal growth. But, also, the church provides fellowship, based on the actions of giving to and receiving from one another.

No one is perfect. Neither is the church perfect. It is made up of sinners saved by grace, who are united with a common bond through faith in Jesus Christ. There is strength, power, and accountability through the bond of fellowship with other believers. Choose a church that presents the gospel in its fullness, a spirit-filled, spirit-led fellowship of believers. Through the church you have protection against teachings that might lead you into false doctrines.

IV.16.2.3.5. Witnessing

Many feel uncomfortable in witnessing (or testifying) about their faith. They feel uncertain about how to do it and what to say. Jesus never promised comfort or ease. He did say, *"ye shall be witnesses unto me"* (Acts 1:8). This was his last exhortation to his disciples before he ascended to heaven. *"And when he had spoken these things ... he was taken up"* (Acts 1:9). His last words were to be witnesses.

Your words don't have to be filled with eloquent phrases and lofty terminology. In your own words, tell what you have experienced and what you have become. Consider the blind man healed by Jesus in John 9. The Pharisees brought the man in to question him about his healing, hoping to prove, through this man's testimony (witness) that Jesus was a sinner. When asked to testify about Christ, his response was simplistic yet powerfully eloquent. *"Whether he is a sinner or not, I don't know. One thing I do know. I was blind but now I see!"* (John 9:25, NIV) Tell what God has done for you. Let the Holy Spirit do the rest.

For most people in the world, personal witnessing is the only way they will ever know about salvation through faith in Jesus Christ. There are many who will never go to a church service or an evangelistic crusade. These people need to know that Jesus saves. Many will die in their sins unless someone takes the gospel message to them personally. What about the person who sits next to you on a bus or airplane? What about the person who teaches your children? What about the person who lives next to you? If you don't tell them, who will?

You witness by your actions as well as your words. Do not think people will not watch you. Your life should be a testimony of the grace that God has shown you. If the world shows love, your love should be deeper and stronger. If the world shows compassion, your compassion should be greater than all others. As you witness for Christ, you will grow in your relationship with him.

IV.16.2.4. Follow-Up

Up to this point we have discussed what believers can do for personal growth. Now, we turn our focus to how that can be used to disciple others, helping them to grow in their relationship with Christ. First, and foremost, never forget that new believers are just that – new believers. Many will have no idea what faith in Christ is all about, nor about how that impacts their lives. If they have any knowledge about the church at all it is probably based on negative childhood memories or how the media has portrayed Christians (which is usually not very attractive or positive). Very few will be starting with no pre-conceived ideas about Christianity. You will have to break down the walls and barriers that may have been there, helping them to understand exactly what has happened to them and what they can and will become. Be patient. Be diligent. They are not mature. They need love and understanding. Most importantly, they need to be taught what to do with their new faith.

In the "Principles of global Evangelism" lessons we discussed steps for follow-up after a crusade. The initial contact by individuals from the local church should be friendly and welcoming. The new converts should not be overwhelmed with a lot of tedious information about changing their lifestyle.

IV.16.2.4.1. Personal Contact

The personal contact can be made by a phone call, a brief visit, or a note of some sort. The brief visit is, by far, the best option, but if that's not feasible, a phone call will, at least, set the stage for future dialogue. A hand written note of encouragement, though nice, is not the best venue for making the initial contact.

Phone call: a phone call is best used to let the person know how excited you are for him and to schedule a time when you can get together. It's highly unlikely the new believer will unburden his soul in a phone call immediately following his salvation experience. The call will be more of a personal contact of encouragement.

Brief visit: the "visit" is the best way to demonstrate support of the individual in his new faith. Be careful, however, that the new believer is not overwhelmed by too many visits (or calls). The first visit should be brief, establishing lines of communication, offering assistance, answering questions but not delving into difficult issues. There will be plenty of time for that. If the new believer does not have a Bible, this would be a good time to give him one. Suggest he start reading the gospel of John. (Caution him against randomly picking a passage to read. It can be very discouraging if he opens the Bible and starts reading a more difficult book like Leviticus.) Make yourself available to answer questions he might have as he reads John. Encourage him to come to church with you. Offer to meet him there. He needs reassurance that nothing weird or uncomfortable is about to happen. Before leaving, set a time to get together, at his convenience, to talk more.

Note or card: a note or card is best used as a follow-up to your initial contact and as a point of encouragement when you aren't able to make a personal call or visit. The note can simply state that you are thinking and praying for the person and that you are available if he wants to talk about anything.

Show love: the person making the contact should be warm and personable. Tell the new believer how happy you are for the decision he has made. Offer to answer any questions he might have about what salvation means. This first contact is not the time to launch into a long study of biblical theology. The new believer is not ready for that. Right now, he needs to know the love of brothers and sisters in Christ and understand that he has people who will support him and help him to grow. Too much information too soon can frighten new believers and many will give up if they feel there is no way they can live up to what is expected of them as Christians.

The new believer is going to be feeling a sense of joy, but also a sense of apprehension. He doesn't know what this new life in Christ means. Be careful using cliché terms; they mean nothing to him. Advise him that the euphoria he feels will diminish, in time; then reassure him that doesn't change who he is in Christ.

Do not judge: refrain from judging new believers based on their economic or social status; don't be guilty of showing favoritism to one individual over another. The new believer will have to make changes. He will inevitably stumble. Certainly, there are some issues that will have to be addressed, but don't become so legalistic in the law that the new believer is unable to bear the pressure.

IV.16.2.4.2. Invitation to Church / Fellowship

New believers need to be taught the fundamentals of Christianity. They also need the support of the community of believers that can come through the church. After an individual has become a believer, that individual needs to find a church home. Many new believers will not know where to go or what to do. They will probably feel uncomfortable going into a church they have never been to before. It is crucial that you do all you can to make them feel comfortable, at home and a part.

Don't wait for the new believers to come to the church. Go to them. Invite them to a service. Encourage them to bring their spouse and/or children. Offer to stop by their home to go with them, or meet them at the church. Make sure they know the service time, appropriate attire and what they can expect. If you are taking them to a full-gospel church where the gifts of the Spirit will be in evidence, prepare them for that. If they have never heard someone speak in tongues, that may be a frightening or discomforting experience. Do all you can to make them comfortable with their first-time church experience. If you are meeting them at the church, tell them exactly where you will be and then be there. Be there early. Once there, introduce them to other believers – especially other believers who might share common interests with the new believer. For example, if a believer is a young married, introduce him to other young marrieds who are of the same age. If they have brought children, make sure the children are also taken care of and that the new believers meet the people who are working in the children's area.

If you were not able to introduce the new believers to the pastor before the service, make sure you do so afterwards. Offer to take them out for coffee or to get something to eat following the service so you can answer any questions they might have. Explain the opportunities for ministry and involvement at the church, but don't push them to commit to a ministry. Give them time to get used to the whole idea of church involvement.

One caution should be noted here. Often churches are so excited about new believers that they try to get them involved in too many things too quickly – especially before the new believers are emotionally and spiritually ready. The church is not intentionally doing something bad; it's just that their eagerness to get the new believer involved may become a stumbling block for the new believer's stability. Someone who is strong in the Lord should be there to guide the new believer in his quest for spiritual growth and, eventually, church involvement.

Evangelist Bonnke cautions against becoming so busy that we do not have time for what is essential. If the new believer becomes so busy through involvement at the church that he is not able to devote time to his personal growth (Bible study, meditation, prayer, etc.), then he has his priorities in the wrong order and his walk with God will surely suffer.

When Paul said he could do all things through Christ, he did not mean that he did all things himself, running around in church work like a cat on hot bricks ... Jesus did not mean us to work all hours that come and take on a multitude of concerns and responsibilities.

We can be too busy, always rushing about on some business or other, with so many irons in the fire it almost puts the fire out; we do not have time for what Jesus says is necessary. *"Whoever believes will not act hastily"* (Isaiah 28:16).

For the new believer, what is necessary is time to grow and understand who he is in Christ, to gain insight into what the Bible is saying and to learn how to apply Biblical truths to his own life. This is the important necessary part of a new believer's new life.

IV.16.2.5. Discipleship of New Believers

The new believer has been contacted and has been brought into the local church. At this point the true discipleship training begins. Do not assume the new believer has a clear understanding of Christianity. Do not assume the new believer has a clear understanding of what it means to serve God. Do not assume the new believer has a clear understanding of what are appropriate lifestyle habits within the community of believers. Now, that he is saved, it is time to take this rough gem and polish it into a refined jewel. That's what discipleship is all about.

It should be noted that when someone is discipling another person, the person doing the discipleship training should be a more spiritually mature individual. It is unwise to let a relatively new convert disciple another new convert. Certainly, someone who is newer to the faith may be able to relate to the new believer's struggles, but there is no substitute for the wisdom of one who is seasoned and mature in his relationship with the Lord. Paul's relationship with Timothy serves as a good example of a discipleship relationship.

IV.16.2.5.1. Teaching

"Train up a child in the way he should go; and when he is old, he will not depart from it" (Proverbs 22:6). This is our instruction on how we

should train (teach) our children. It is applicable in the nurturing
and training of new believers. In essence, new believers are children
- spiritual children. They have to be taught everything they have
to know to grow into mature Christians. Start with small, easy to
understand concepts and build on those.

There is so much that a new believer needs to be taught. He needs to
know how to study the Bible. He needs to know how to find guidance,
strength and power for each day. He needs to know how to lead a
successful Christian life.

IV.16.2.5.2. Bible Study

All the teaching you can do will be ineffective if it is not grounded in
the Word of God. In addition to lifestyle teaching, new believers need
to receive clear instruction in the Bible itself, finding the Bible is their
guidebook for this new life they have before them. As they grow in
their knowledge and understanding of the Word, they will become
more adept at applying the Word to their own lives. This is more than
listening to the preached Word. Through Bible study they are able to
look more closely at the specifics of the Word, the background and
application. Encourage new believers to get into a good Bible study
program. Perhaps a Sunday School class or a specific study program
offered through the local church could be available for them. If the
church does not offer those options, it should. Other options might
be a good home fellowship study program. Not one that is purely
social in scope; rather, one that uses the environment of fellowship
coupled with the intensity of deliberate study. New believers will need
mentors who can help them research and study the Word, rightly
divided. The mentor should observe with caution lest the new believer
become entangled in study that is not biblically based or sound.

Module IV
Lesson 17
The Holy Spirit and Evangelism

References: *Mighty Manifestations*

"But ye shall receive power, after that the Holy Ghost [Holy Spirit] *is come upon you: and ye shall be witnesses unto me both in Jerusalem, and in all Judea, and in Samaria, and unto the uttermost part of the earth"* (Acts 1:8). These were the last recorded words of Jesus Christ before he ascended into heaven at the end of his three years of earthly ministry. Important to note is that he spoke of both Holy Spirit anointing and evangelism. It wasn't an either/or situation. You **shall** receive power and you **shall** be witnesses. His last charge to his followers was two-fold: he promised power and he declared their mission.

"The anointing of the Lord is a thorough-soaking baptism. Anointing with the Holy Spirit and fire is not intended to be for one aspect of human life or one function; it is an immersion of the whole personality in the element of God's Spirit. When a cloth is dipped in a dye ("baptized" means "dipped"), the cloth takes on the nature of the dye. When we are "dipped" into the element of the Holy Spirit, we take on his nature."

IV.17.1.   Who Is the Holy Spirit?

The terms "Holy Spirit" and "Holy Ghost" are used interchangeably in scripture to reference the third person of the Trinity, or Godhead, i.e., Father, Son, Holy Spirit. *"Go ye therefore, and teach all nations, baptizing them in the name of the Father, and of the Son, and of the Holy Ghost"* (Matthew 28:19). There is only one God. God is Father, God is Son and God is Holy Spirit. All three are God and all three are one. *"For there are three that bear record in heaven, the Father, the Word* [Son], *and the Holy Ghost: and these three are one"* (1 John 5:7).

In Matthew's account of Jesus' water baptism (Matthew 3:13-17), the Trinity is evidenced through:

Jesus (the Son) - receiving baptism (v.16)
Spirit of God (the Holy Spirit) - descending like a dove (v.16)
Voice from heaven (the Father) - declaring Jesus to be the Son who pleases him (v.17)

The Spirit did the will of the Word and the Word did the will of the Father. The Personalities of the Godhead never operate independently. Jesus said, *"The Son can do nothing of himself, but what he seeth the Father do"* (John 5:19b)

Additional Reading

Read from *Mighty Manifestations*
chapter 2 on pages 203-214 of the book passage compilation

IV.17.2.   Gifts of the Spirit

"Now concerning spiritual gifts, brethren, I would not have you ignorant ... Now there are diversities of gifts, but the same Spirit. And there are differences of administrations, but the same Lord ... But all these worketh that one and the selfsame Spirit, dividing to every man severally as he will" (1 Corinthians 12:1,4,5,11).

In Evangelist Bonnke's discussion of spiritual gifts in *Mighty Manifestations*, he notes, "The gifts of the Spirit never designate natural talents, such as a gift for music, or art ... The gifts in 1 Corinthians 12 are supernatural, manifestations of the Spirit". He continues by expounding on Paul's explanation of why the gifts differ from person to person. Paul described the church as a body with many members, each member uniquely different, yet having a vital role in the function of the body. Though some parts may differ in their function, each is necessary and none should be perceived as having more importance than another. So it is with the gifts of the Spirit. Each is manifested according to need and purpose. Some receive one gift, others a different gift. No one gift should be esteemed higher than another; no one gift should be considered less important that the rest (1 Corinthians 12:14-31).

The emphasis should not be on the gift, lest the gift become an idol. The recipient of the gift should not glory in his gift, lest the gift become a stumbling block of self-pride. The use of one gift should not be exalted over another, lest the gifts cause jealousy, division, and strife. Ultimately all gifts must be related to and operational toward the purposes of God for redemption.

Let us consider each of the gifts mentioned in 1 Corinthians 12:8-10. *"For to one is given by the Spirit the word of wisdom; to another the word of knowledge by the same Spirit; To another faith by the same Spirit; to another the gifts of healing by the same Spirit; To another the working of miracles; to another prophecy; to another discerning of spirits; to another divers kinds of tongues; to another the interpretation of tongues."*

IV.17.2.1. Word of Wisdom

A word of wisdom is a supernatural wisdom not gained through education. It refers to the wisdom of God and is that ability to use knowledge and determine how to act in any situation, to the glory of God. James 1:5 tells us that it is available to all.

"The gift of the word of wisdom is God at the wheel keeping us heading in the right direction even when we are busy in matters that seem remote". The practicality of a word of wisdom is noted in its timing and application. It is not necessarily a proclamation given in the context of a church service. It could quite simply be a part of an independent discussion during which the Holy Spirit prompts someone to reveal divine truth or insight. Or, it might be a revelation that occurs during a time of Bible study, prayer or meditation when the Holy Spirit reveals Scripture that has application to specific circumstances. It has a practical purpose and may come in a fashion that is neither miraculous nor seems overly religious.

Additional Reading

Read from *Mighty Manifestations*
chapter 7 on pages 223-231 of the book passage compilation

IV.17.2.2. Word of Knowledge

Wisdom and knowledge complement each other. "If a special word [of knowledge] brings to light a particular circumstance, a word of wisdom may well be needed also to do what should be done". Evangelist Bonnke provides four clues that define knowledge.

First, the basic knowledge, to know God, which is
only by revelation through His Son our Lord Jesus
Christ. The Bible calls it 'understanding', which
means a living acquaintance with God. Secondly, a
deeper heart-grasp of His Word. Thirdly, a divinely
inspired sense of what is right and wrong, or wise and
foolish in life. Fourthly, the Father knows all things,
and they that know Him may have His confidence and
share a little of what He sees.

This type of knowledge cannot be obtained by study. It is given by
the Holy Spirit to our human spirit and is to be acted upon by our
renewed mind. It is not a permanent possession; rather, it is essential
for the moment. That is not to say, that "study" is unimportant. Quite
the contrary! Study of the Word prepares our hearts and minds to be
open to receive the word of knowledge through inspiration of the Holy
Spirit. (2 Timothy 2:15) It is divine equipment that is given to enable
us to carry out our part in the Great Commission, to minister in the
light of facts given by the Holy Spirit.

Additional Reading

**Read from *Mighty Manifestations*
chapter 8 on pages 232-242 of the book passage compilation**

Module IV
Lesson 18
The Holy Spirit and Evangelism (continued)

Reference: *Mighty Manifestations*

IV.18.1. Gifts of the Spirit (continued)

IV.18.1.1. Faith

Four kinds of faith can be identified.

1. Common faith – possessed by all men.
2. Saving faith – a gift, as evidenced in Ephesians 2:8
   "For by grace are ye saved through faith: and that not of yourselves: it is the gift of God".
3. Faith – one of the fruit of the Spirit, ever-increasing faith.
4. Faith – an empowerment faith, the gift of the Holy Spirit.

The latter, like the other gifts, is temporary and is enabled to meet the needs of the moment. As with the other gifts, a daily spiritual walk is essential to its operation. It is a manifestation of the Spirit and demonstrates the supernatural might of God. "It is useless to exhort congregations to exercise faith on that level. They cannot have mountain-moving faith just by trying … [it] is not the product of striving, straining, and concentrating. It is rest, not labor."

Additional Reading

Read from *Mighty Manifestations*
chapter 9 on pages 243-254 of the book passage compilation

IV.18.1.2. Healing

Healing is part of God's plan of redemption. *"Who his own self bare our sins in his own body on the tree, that we, being dead to sins, should live unto righteousness: by whose stripes ye were healed"* (1 Peter 2:24). Jesus died for the remission of sins and through his suffering we are healed, spiritually and physically. The operation of this gift is relative to our response, as well as the response of the one for whom we are praying. It comes in response to faith, need, and the will of God.

"The gift of healing is not a commission to heal all and sundry, but only such as the Holy Spirit gives a manifestation for". Correspondingly, the gift of healing for one specific affliction only has no Biblical precedent. Be wary of those who claim such a gift.

Additional Reading

**Read from *Mighty Manifestations*
chapter 10 on pages 255-263
chapter 11 on pages 264-271
of the book passage compilation**

Module IV
Lesson 19
The Holy Spirit and Evangelism (continued)

Reference: *Mighty Manifestations*

IV.19.1.   Gifts of the Spirit (continued)

IV.19.1.1.   Miracles

The phrase "working of miracles" used in 1 Corinthians 12:10 is translated from the Greek (*energemata dunameon*) to mean literally the "operations of powers" and covers a variety of signs and wonders, not specifying one particular miraculous work. Generally, there is a tendency to equate "miracles" with healings and deliverance, as evidenced in Acts 8:6-7. *"And the people with one accord gave heed unto those things which Philip spake, hearing and seeing the miracles which he did. For unclean spirits, crying with loud voice, came out of many that were possessed with them: and many taken with palsies, and that were lame, were healed.* Scripture would indicate that there is more power available. Jesus said, *"He that believeth on me, the works that I do shall he do also; and greater works than these shall he do ..."* (John 14:12). Jesus healed. Jesus delivered. But he said believers would do more. The power is available to us now!

Additional Reading

**Read from *Mighty Manifestations*
chapter 12 on pages 272-280 of the book passage compilation**

IV.19.1.2. Prophecy

The gift of prophecy as noted in this section is prophecy which is a momentary Holy Spirit inspired proclamation. The Holy Spirit gives inspiration to declare, tell, or proclaim truth in a situation or exchange. It is used in ministering to others, without necessarily knowing the need, and is for edification, exhortation and comfort, most often proclaiming rather than predicting. "All prophecy ... should move in that same all-important direction, to focus the hopes, faith, and conduct of us all towards the realization of eternal redemption and the Kingdom."

> While prophecy is not to utter glibly whatever enters our heads any time we fancy, and preface it with 'I, the Lord, do say unto thee', it is also true that the Lord encourages the bold prophet who steps out in faith and initiative. The principle here is that the prophet is the servant of the Holy Spirit. The Spirit is not the servant of a prophet, but the Spirit works *with* the prophet.

A word should be noted here with regard to false prophets or false prophecies. Prophecy has been misused and just because someone claims to have a word from the Lord does not mean it is necessarily true. We must always check prophecies against the Word of God to guard against error.

Additional Reading

**Read from *Mighty Manifestations*
chapter 13 on pages 281-293 of the book passage compilation**

Module IV
Lesson 20
The Holy Spirit and Evangelism (continued)

Reference: *Mighty Manifestations*

IV.20.1. Gifts of the Spirit (continued)

IV.20.1.1 Discernment

The gift of discernment (more accurately "discerning of spirits") is "not a gift to see what is invisible, but the power to judge what is seen, whether good or bad." This gift can save us from deception and is provided to empower us to bring deliverance to others. "The gift of the discerning of spirits will guide us in our walk through dangerous minefields ... leading us into all truth, as Jesus promised."

Additional Reading

Read from *Mighty Manifestations*
chapter 14 on pages 294-302 of the book passage compilation

IV.20.1.2. Tongues and Interpretation

Tongues is an utterance in a language that is unknown to the speaker and is given instantaneously by the Holy Spirit (Acts 2:4; 10:44-46; 19:1-6). It is an earthly or celestial language, spoken only by believers, as the Holy Spirit gives them the ability to do so. When used as a prayer language, the speaker is talking to God, not to men. Tongues are for the unbeliever only if there is an interpretation. The interpretation of tongues is just that, an interpretation, and not a literal word-for-word translation. It works in sequence to any language that is unknown to the hearer. Because of this, interpretation of tongues is the only gift that operates in conjunction with another gift, i.e., tongues.

Additional Reading

**Read from *Mighty Manifestations*
chapter 15 on pages 303-315 of the book passage compilation**

IV.20.2. The Holy Spirit Is the Spirit of ...

IV.20.2.1. Conviction

Conviction of sin is the work of the Holy Spirit and not brought about by condemnation by the evangelist. The evangelist who thinks that he has the power and authority to convict people of their sins is ignorant and preaching a false doctrine. The evangelist is one vehicle whereby the Word is presented. Then, using the Word (written and preached), the Holy Spirit brings conviction into the hearts of those who hear. This is why it is so important that evangelists keep their focus on God, study His Word and submit themselves to His authority, leading and anointing.

It is not in our power to condemn or to save. Don't lose sight of that! Conviction is brought to fruition through a veritable symphony of experiences, all combined to orchestrate the convicting recognition of an individual's own sinful nature. Each of us is part of that symphony. If any of us fails to do his part, the symphony is incomplete. That doesn't mean conviction cannot come. Nevertheless, an individual's receptivity to the convicting power of the Holy Spirit may be lessened when we fail to do our part in proclaiming the gospel message of redemption through the blood of Jesus Christ.

"Nevertheless I tell you the truth; It is expedient for you that I go away; for if I go not away the Comforter [Holy Spirit] will not come unto you. And when he is come, he will reprove the world of sin, and of righteousness, and of judgment: Of sin, because they believe not on me; Of righteousness, because I go to my Father, and ye see me no more; Of judgment, because the prince of this world is judged" (John 16:7-11).

IV.20.2.2. Power

The evangelist must pray and seek Holy Spirit power for his ministry. He needs power in three ways. Power within himself, to be able to do the work to which he has been called. Power upon the message, that the words he speaks will be full of Holy Spirit power and truth. Power upon the listener, that he would be receptive to hear the words spoken through the anointing of the Holy Spirit.

Jesus called us to be witnesses, but He didn't just throw us into the midst of the lost without assistance. The Holy Spirit (the Comforter) has come to empower us to preach the gospel, anointing us to proclaim the love of Christ and the remission of sins that is available to all who believe. Without the Holy Spirit power, our words would be ineffective and effete. They would lack that spark that ignites the embers of faith within the hearts of those seeking forgiveness. We must have the power of the Holy Spirit to be effective. We dare not go forth without it.

"Now the God of hope fill you with all joy and peace in believing, that ye may abound in hope, through the power of the Holy Ghost ... Through mighty signs and wonders, by the power of the Spirit of God" (Romans 15:13,19a).

IV.20.2.3. Faith

Earlier, in our discussion on the gifts of the Holy Spirit, we talked about "saving faith." It is not within your power or control to save anyone. Saving faith is the gift of the Holy Spirit. The evangelist must

pray for the Holy Spirit to grant this work of grace. Pray for faith
within the hearts of the listeners to believe and to receive. Similarly,
the evangelist must use his faith to step forth to do the work for which
he has been called. "If our faith does not push us into action it is not
worth much. We show our faith by our deeds ... A man of faith will do
what others would never attempt".

IV.20.2.4. Holiness

The Holy Spirit works in the new believer to change his life.
Sometimes the change is instantaneous. Other times, the change is a
progression over time. Nevertheless, as a believer (new or old) seeks
to know the Lord better and strives to serve Him, the Holy Spirit
will bring to his mind those things in his life that are displeasing to
God. In many respects this is a second act of conviction – conviction
of lifestyle – which leads the believer into a life of holiness that is
pleasing to God.

As others watch our lives, they should see in us a life that is dedicated
to service, non-compromising in its commitment to faith in Christ,
and exemplary in its holiness of lifestyle. That is not to say we should
all sequester ourselves away from the world for fear we will be tainted
by worldly sin. Quite the contrary! Through the strength and power
of the Holy Spirit we are to be lights in the darkness, leading others to
a life of repentance and salvation through Jesus Christ. Others should
see in us a life to be desired.

*"There is therefore now no condemnation to them which are in Christ
Jesus, who walk not after the flesh, but after the Spirit"* (Romans 8:1).

IV.20.3. Jesus Commanded the Disciples to Tarry / Pentecost

Jesus knew his disciples would need help as they went forth to proclaim the gospel. This was the same group who just weeks before had run away in fear at Gethsemane and had cowered in fearful seclusion following the crucifixion. This was the same group who had failed to grasp the simplest of illustrations and argued over who would be greater in the Kingdom. Jesus knew they would need help. He did not send them forth immediately; rather, he told them to tarry in Jerusalem until they had received power (Luke 24:49).

Even though he had been with the disciples for the three years of his earthly ministry, Jesus, in his omniscience, knew they were not ready for the things that were to come. He knew what they were to face. He knew they needed more. They were to tarry.

How difficult that must have been for this brash group of rugged and, at times, impetuous and impatient fishermen! They had witnessed the singular most important event in the history of mankind – redemption through the death and resurrection of the Son of God. He had told them they were to be fishers of men. He had told them they would do greater things than he had done. He had told them they would go into all the world and preach the gospel and that they would be followed by signs and wonders. Devils would be cast out! They would speak with new tongues. Neither serpents nor deadly drink would hurt them. They would lay hands on the sick and the sick would be healed. (Mark 16:15-18) Yet, now, he was telling them to tarry ... to wait! To wait for what? They did not know. Jesus had said, "Go" and now he was saying, "Wait!"

So, they waited. And they waited. And they waited. And, finally ... *"when the day of Pentecost was fully come, they were all with one accord in one place. And suddenly there came a sound from heaven as of a rushing mighty wind, and it filled all the house where they were sitting.*

And there appeared unto them cloven tongues like as of fire, and it sat upon each of them. And they were all filled with the Holy Ghost, and began to speak with other tongues, as the Spirit gave them utterance" (Acts 2:1-4).

It's quite certain this is not what they were expecting. It was, however, what they needed. Following Pentecost, the disciples were emboldened and empowered as never before. They took the gospel to the world and the world was changed as never before, and as nothing since. Peter, who had denied Christ, now stood boldly declaring that Jesus was the resurrected Son of God. Peter, who had often acted with haste, now preached with anointing and power. Three thousand souls were saved that day. Not because of Peter, but because of the convicting power of the Holy Spirit, anointing Peter to preach and quickening the hearts of those who heard. This was the power of Pentecost then! It is still the power of Pentecost today!

Talent, ability and education are no substitute for the power of the Holy Spirit. Evangelists must pray and fast until the Holy Spirit power is operative in their lives. That is not to say talent, ability and education are unimportant. The evangelist should do all he can to improve his talent, perfect his abilities, and gain as much education as possible. Having done all that, however, without the anointing of the Holy Spirit, they are powerless.

"The anointing of the Spirit is as much physical as spiritual. The tongues of fire on the day of Pentecost were a visible expression of God and man coming together ... The Holy Spirit is God exclusive to this earth and to mankind. That is the core revolution of Pentecost. It restores the truth of salvation being for body and soul, linking both orders in human experience."

IV.20.4. Inviting Seekers to Receive the Holy Spirit

In addition to preaching for salvation, the full gospel evangelist must occasionally urge the congregations to seek and receive the Holy Spirit themselves. Baptism in the Holy Spirit is a special experience for believers beyond salvation. It is given for power and anointing and new believers should be invited to seek the power that comes through the Holy Spirit. "God does not give His gifts to the unconverted, nor His Holy Spirit to the world, but when we are born again we are encouraged to be filled, just as Paul admonished the churches". For every believer, Paul's admonition in Ephesians 5:18 (*"Be filled with the Spirit"*) is still true today. New believers may not understand and the evangelist should teach and lead them into a full understanding of the meaning of baptism in the Holy Spirit and its blessings and benefits to them.

Preach the Pentecostal blessing! Help those who are under your teaching and preaching to grow in their relationship with the Lord and to find complete fulfillment of all of His promises to them. Tell them, teach them, train them. The blessing is theirs for the asking. How can they ask if they do not know to do so? The power that you have received through the Holy Spirit is not yours to keep. You must guide others to receive the same power. If you do not lead them, who will?

The scriptures given below illustrate the promise of the outpouring of the Holy Spirit, its fulfillment at Pentecost and its subsequent outpouring to other believers, Jew and Gentile. This experience was readily accepted by the early Christian church and is still in effect today. All believers are entitled to the blessing and should seek the fulfillment of the promise of the baptism in the Holy Spirit and fire. With this blessing comes power for life, service and ministry.

Luke 11:13: *"If ye then, being evil, know how to give good gifts unto your children: how much more shall your heavenly Father give the Holy Spirit to them that ask him?"*

Acts 1:4-5a,8: *"And being assembled together with them, commanded them that they should not depart from Jerusalem, but wait for the promise of the Father, which, saith he, ye have heard of me. For John truly baptized with water; but ye shall be baptized with the Holy Ghost ... But ye shall receive power, after that the Holy Ghost is come upon you: and ye shall be witnesses unto me both in Jerusalem, and in all Judea, and in Samaria, and unto the uttermost part of the earth."*

Acts 2:1,4: *"And when the day of Pentecost was fully come, they were all with one accord in one place ... And they were all filled with the Holy Ghost, and began to speak with other tongues, as the Spirit gave them utterance."*

Acts 8:15-17: *"Who, when they were come down, prayed for them, that they might receive the Holy Ghost: (For as yet he was fallen upon none of them: only they were baptized in the name of the Lord Jesus.) Then laid they their hands on them, and they received the Holy Ghost."*

Acts 10:44-46a: *"While Peter yet spake these words, the Holy Ghost fell on all them which heard the word. And they of the circumcision which believed were astonished, as many as came with Peter, because that on the Gentiles also was poured out the gift of the Holy Ghost. For they heard them speak with tongues, and magnify God."*

Acts 11:15-16: *"And as I began to speak, the Holy Ghost fell on them, as on us at the beginning. Then remembered I the word of the Lord, how that he said, John indeed baptized with water; but ye shall be baptized with the Holy Ghost."*

Acts 15:7-9: *"Peter rose up, and said unto them, Men and brethren, ye know how that a good while ago God made choice among us, that the Gentiles by my mouth should hear the word of the gospel, and believe. And God which knoweth the hearts, bare them witness, giving them the*

Holy Ghost, even as he did unto us; And put no difference between us and them, purifying their hearts by faith."

Acts 19:2,6: *"And he said unto them, Have ye received the Holy Ghost since ye believed? And they said unto him, We have not so much as heard whether there be any Holy Ghost ... And when Paul had laid his hands upon them, the Holy Ghost came on them; and they spake with tongues, and prophesied."*

Additional Reading

Read from chapter 2 of *Mighty Manifestations*
***The Effect of the Spirit* on pages 212-214**
of the book passage compilation

"The grace of the Lord Jesus Christ, and the love of God,
and the communion of the Holy Ghost, be with you all. Amen."
2 Corinthians 13:14

"If it looks like a baptism, sounds like it, feels like it,
operates like it, what else is it?"
Reinhard Bonnke

Overview of additional Reading

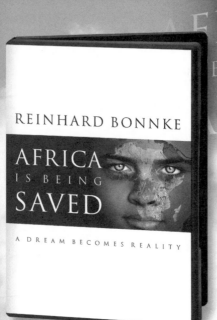

Africa is being saved
2 DVD Set

Through crusades in Nigeria and throughout the African continent, evangelist Reinhard Bonnke and his Christ for all Nations team have discovered the incredible joy of seeing millions of souls dedicated to Jesus. Now, in this captivating double DVD collection, you too can experience firsthand how God is bringing salvation and healing to his People. Listen, watch, and enjoy – you'll soon be inspired to join in this amazing movement of miracles!

DVD 1:   Music Video "Broken and beautiful" by Mark Schulz
Behind the scenes documentary "Africa is being saved"
Bonus Rap MP3 "Africa shall be saved" by Artist Harry

DVD 2:   Sermon Fire Conference "Go into all the World"
Sermon Crusade "The rich Man and Lazarus"

Total running time approx. 4 hours • ISBN 978-1-933106-65

Holy Spirit
Revelation & Revolution

Trying to write about the Holy Spirit is like trying to dive to the depths of the ocean with just a snorkel. The deeper you go the more beautiful it becomes, yet reaching the bottom is impossible. This book by the renowned Evangelist Reinhard Bonnke is the best writing on the Holy Spirit, the third Person of the Godhead that one has ever read. It is not a mere personal opinion, but a revelation of unchangeable truths grounded in biblical facts. The author writes from over 40 years of practical experience of the reality of the Holy Spirit. Over 100 years ago a new move of the Holy Spirit spread from Los Angeles to Scandinavia and on into Europe. May this book ignite each and every reader to experience what God has promised to every Christian serious about serving God. Here is profound truth so simple that even a child can understand it, yet revelation so deep that it will challenge every scholar to look afresh at a revolutionary new dimension of the Holy Spirit.

172 pages • ISBN 978-1-933106-62-5

Hell empty Heaven full

Every day, millions of people move farther down the dark road to destruction. They are your coworkers, your neighbors, your friends – and they are *lost*.

Yet one individual, arms outstretched in the shape of a cross, stands in the middle of that road, blocking their way. His name is Jesus. And one person at a time, He is turning the crowd around, gently pointing each toward an eternity of hope and joy.

Millions of people in our world today are reaching out for an answer to their desperation. As believers, we are called to deliver these lost souls to heaven. No one man or woman can save them all – yet when we partner with Jesus, the "impossible" becomes possible. The 21st-century Christian church is expanding rapidly. One in every ten people already follows Christ. Our goal is in sight!

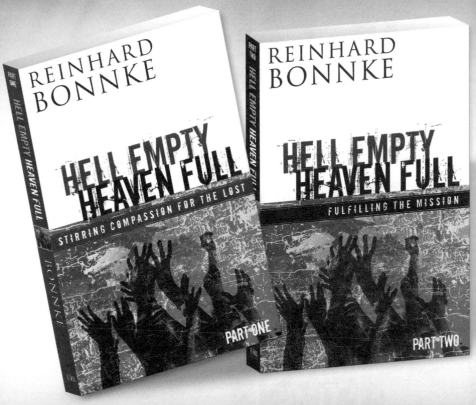

In *Hell Empty Heaven Full* – part one and two – author and international evangelist Reinhard Bonnke shares his personal passion for bringing the gospel to every one of God's children. He invites you – he *urges* you – to join Jesus at the crossroads between despair and delight. There isn't a moment to lose. Hell was never designed for the lost. Heaven is expecting them!

Part 1 • 192 pages • ISBN 978-1-933106-56-4
Part 2 • 184 pages • ISBN 978-1-933106-57-1

Evangelism by Fire

Igniting Your Passion for the Lost

Evangelism by Fire will give you an insight into the God-inspired anointing of Reinhard Bonnke. This book will fire your faith and give you the encouragement to believe God for the impossible. Evangelism by Fire is a powerful and practical presentation of the principles which the Lord has taught him over the years.

320 pages • ISBN 3-935057-19-9

Audiobook
10 CDs • ISBN 0-9758789-2-1

Workbook
88 pages • ISBN 3-935057-28-8

Time is running out

There are more lost souls than ever – and less time than ever to save them. Now the evangelist's evangelist calls us – and helps us – to redouble our efforts to win over the world for Jesus. Reinhard Bonnke's unbridled passion for winning souls dates back to his youth. He is acclaimed worldwide for a ministry that has one avowed, all-consuming purpose – plunder hell to populate heaven! Poignant, exhorting and uncompromising, this dramatic book combines the author's excitement for evangelism with his proven, effective techniques for reaching the lost of this world. It is a resounding call for each of us to reexamine our priorities, heed the call of Christ, preach the good news, and save people from hell.

252 pages • ISBN 3-935057-60-1

Workbook
88 pages • ISBN 3-935057-85-7

Works Cited

The page and chapter references used refer to hard copies of the
following 4 books by Evangelist Reinhard Bonnke (see pages 150-151):

Evangelism By Fire
Full Flame GmbH ©2002, Edition 8, Frankfurt, Germany

Mighty Manifestations
Full Flame GmbH ©2002, Edition 2, Frankfurt, Germany

Faith - The Link With God's Power
Full Flame GmbH ©2003, Edition 7, Frankfurt, Germany

Time Is Running Out
Full Flame GmbH ©2003, Edition 2, Frankfurt, Germany

Cfan CHRIST FOR ALL NATIONS

To contact Christ for all Nations, the ministry of Evangelist Reinhard Bonnke, please use this information:

www.cfan.org

North America
Christ for all Nations
P.O. Box 590588
Orlando, Florida 32859-0588
U.S.A.

Latin America
Christ for all Nations
Caixa Postal 10360
Curibita – PR
80.730-970
Brazil

Southern Africa
Christ for all Nations
P O Box 50015
West Beach, 7449
South Africa

Canada
Christ for all Nations
P.O. Box 25057
London, Ontario
N6C 6A8

Continental Europe
Christus für alle Nationen
Postfach 60 05 95
60335 Frankfurt am Main
Germany

United Kingdom
Christ for all Nations
250 Coombs Road
Halesowen
West Midlands, B62 8AA
United Kingdom

Asia
Christ for all Nations
Asia/Pacific
Singapore Post Centre Post Office
P.O. Box 418
Singapore 914014

Australia
Christ for all Nations
Locked Bag 50
Burleigh Town
Queensland 4220
Australia

SOUTHEASTERN UNIVERSITY
Gathered in the Spirit.
Equipping for every good work.

THE REINHARD BONNKE
SCHOOL OF FIRE

For information on the *Reinhard Bonnke School of Fire* and on
effective training for soul-winning and evangelism, please contact us at:

www.schooloffire.com
info@schooloffire.com

or directly at:

The Reinhard Bonnke School of Fire
P.O. Box 593647
Orlando, Florida 32859
U.S.A.

PRODUCTIONS
Evangelistic Resources

For ordering Reinhard Bonnke products, please visit our website
www.e-r-productions.com

We also carry a wide range of **products in other languages**,
such as German, Spanish, Portuguese, French ...

Please contact your local office for other languages:

North America & Canada	**Europe**	**Asia & Australia**
E-R Productions LLC	E-R Productions GmbH	E-R Productions Asia Pte Ltd.
P.O. Box 593647	Postfach 60 05 95	451 Joo Chiat Road
Orlando, Florida 32859	60335 Frankfurt am Main	#03-05 Breezeway in Katong
U.S.A.	Germany	Singapore 427664

Latin America	**Southern Africa**
E-R Productions Ltda	E-R Productions RSA
Avenida Sete de Setembro	c/o Revival Tape and Book
4615, 15 Andar	Centre
Batel, Curitiba	P. O. Box 50015
PR 80240-000	West Beach, 7449
Brazil	South Africa

Mighty Manifestations

The Gifts and Power of the Holy Spirit

This book gives us a 'back to the Bible' examination of the spiritual gifts listed in 1 Corinthians 12. These are not given so that we may congratulate ourselves, or polish up our church's images, but to endorse the preaching of the Gospel to those around us. This is a book not only to increase our understanding, but to energise us for action.

298 pages • ISBN 3-935057-00-8

Workbook
72 pages • ISBN 3-935057-27-X

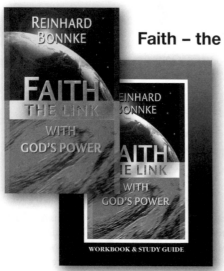

Faith – the Link with God's Power

Some believe that simply having faith is an entitlement to blessing and prosperity. Others believe that faith in oneself is all that is needed in life. Still others contend that faith is a cosmic force that breeds superhuman, super-spiritual, invincible people. In this book, Reinhard Bonnke reveals the truth about faith towards God, drawing from his many years of personal study and experience.

292 pages • ISBN 3-935057-29-6

Workbook
72 pages • ISBN 3-935057-26-1

*All text books are accompanied by **workbooks** as study guide – for your personal use, Sunday school or study groups. They will enable you to work out the truth and practical applications of having a vital and dynamic faith for yourself, as well as gaining deeper insights into the work and ministry of the Holy Spirit in relation to your personal life. These workbooks are a must for each reader of the text book!*